WINGS OF GLORY

BY DERMOT O'LEARY

TOTO THE NINJA CAT
AND THE GREAT SNAKE ESCAPE

TOTO THE NINJA CAT
AND THE INCREDIBLE CHEESE HEIST

TOTO THE NINJA CAT
AND THE SUPERSTAR CATASTROPHE

TOTO THE NINJA CAT
AND THE MYSTERY JEWEL THIEF

TOTO THE NINJA CAT
AND THE LEGEND OF THE WILDCAT

DERMOT O'LEARY

WINGS OF GLORY

ILLUSTRATED BY
CLAIRE POWELL

HODDER CHILDREN'S BOOKS

First published in Great Britain in 2023 by Hodder & Stoughton
This paperback edition first published in 2024

1 3 5 7 9 10 8 6 4 2

Text copyright © Dermot O'Leary, 2023
Illustrations copyright © Claire Powell, 2023

The moral rights of the author and illustrator have been asserted.

A CIP catalogue record for this book
is available from the British Library.

ISBN 978 1 444 96163 8

Printed and bound in Great Britain by Clays Ltd, Elcograf S.p.A.

The paper and board used in this book
are made from wood from responsible sources

Hodder Children's Books
An imprint of
Hachette Children's Group
Part of Hodder & Stoughton Limited
Carmelite House
50 Victoria Embankment
London EC4Y 0DZ

An Hachette UK Company
www.hachette.co.uk

www.hachettechildrens.co.uk

To 'The Few',

who came from near and far.

With eternal gratitude.

Prologue

A long time ago, but not so long that we've forgotten, a war broke out in Europe – and then the world.

It was the second time that a great world war had happened, so it was called the Second World War. No one had believed that such a terrible thing could happen again, and then it did.

It was 1939, and the leader of Germany, Adolf Hitler, had decided that he wanted more land and power for himself. Over the next six years, he would stop at nothing to get it, invading the countries around him and persecuting people without mercy.

At home, ordinary people prepared themselves for the hardships of war that lay ahead, while young sons and daughters headed off to join the Allied forces and fight the enemy armies who wanted to take over the world.

But, still unknown to most of us today, our animal friends also joined the war effort: helping humans in the skies, at sea and on the battlegrounds.

And in 1940, one small bird, barely the weight of an egg, was about to help shape the history of the world . . .

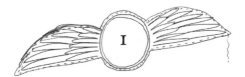

I

'Bandits at two thousand feet below! Look lively and be ready to follow me to intercept!'

Linus's orders cut through the rushing headwind like a dagger. Each one of the birds under his command answered 'Roger!' in unison, and, keeping in perfect formation, waited for his next command.

Linus, a tiny swift from the green fields of England, was squadron leader of an elite fighting unit of peregrine falcons, the fastest and most famous birds in the whole of the Royal Bird Force. They had said it couldn't be done: a little swift commanding the best of the RBF, but here he was, at the head of his loyal unit who would follow him to battle and back.

He looked down at the formation of enemy bombers just

skirting the tops of the white fluffy clouds, heading for the British coastline, and smiled to himself. They wouldn't know what had hit them.

'Tally ho, follow me!' he cried, banking into a steep dive towards his quarry.

Moving as one, his squadron followed. Flying at almost two hundred miles per hour, the falcons and their leader made the distance in no time. They levelled off, undetected, flying just above the lumbering enemy bombers.

Directly below them, Linus could see that the lead plane, a Junkers 88, had its window open. The pilot was looking around, maybe trying to determine his exact location.

Linus knew exactly what to do. 'Squadron, begin intercept!' he ordered.

He dived next to the pilot's window, then suddenly banked right so that he flew straight into the cramped cockpit. Before the pilot had a chance to wonder what on earth was happening, the small bird landed on his head and, using his tiny claws, pulled the pilot's flying helmet over his eyes. The cockpit descended into utter chaos, the pilot trying his best to control the plane, which was lurching all over the skies, and the crew screaming and climbing

over each other, trying to shoo the pesky intruder away.

Gleefully flapping around to cause as much chaos as he could, Linus finally flew out of the cockpit, soaring steeply to safety. Looking back, he saw with delight that his team had followed his lead and every bomber in the formation was now either banking, diving or climbing. The whole German squadron was in complete disarray. As his squadron flew back to join him one by one, he heard the welcome sound of a Rolls-Royce Merlin engine and turned to see the imposing sight of a squadron of friendly Hurricanes coming over the cliffs to intercept the bombers. The slower enemy planes were now scattered and vulnerable, and the birds watched with satisfaction as the RAF either shot down or chased off the last of the enemy.

'Well, Squadron Leader, sir, you've done it again!' exclaimed one of his wingmen. 'There's not a finer bird in the RBF. It's an honour to fly with you, Linus. Linus . . . LINUS!'

'LINUS! Wake up! You have to come and see this!'

Ten thousand feet above the plains of central Africa, Linus was asleep on the wing, in the very clever way that swifts can, gliding on the rising air of the warm thermals. Half his brain was awake, alert and making sure he wasn't tumbling out of the sky, but the other half was very much asleep, enjoying his favourite dream of being an RBF ace.

That is, until his big sister Ava gave his wing a nip with her beak that, quite rudely in his opinion, woke him up.

'Hey! That's the quickest swift-wing on two continents you're biting,' he said, yawning.

She rolled her eyes and banked away, barrel-rolling as she played with the currents. She didn't disagree though. Her brother was cocky, but he was right.

'You might be the fastest swift in the skies around here, but you definitely don't have the sharpest eyes. Look down there at the watering hole. Something's going on. Come on, let's check it out!' With that, she flew into a steep dive towards the ground.

'What do you mean? I've got good eyes! They're just a little small . . . Ava, wait for me, I'm coming!' Linus yelled over the wind, then turned his gaze to the dry earth beneath them.

A large crowd of animals had gathered around the watering hole they called home – and Ava was already halfway there.

'Hey! I said wait for me! You're supposed to be the responsible one!' Linus pinned his wings back and went after her.

Alongside the peregrine falcons, the swifts were considered the fastest birds on the planet. Sure, the golden eagles were quick, the albatrosses could put a shift in, and there was even talk of a spur-winged goose that was pretty nippy, but for out-and-out speed, it was all about the swifts and the falcons. Linus and Ava came from a long line of famous racers. Their grandfather Ernest had won the Paris to Dakar air race a record seven times, and everyone thought Linus had the potential to be even faster when he was older.

Linus caught up with his sister and gave her a friendly bump on the wing, then the swifts fluttered around the crop of trees that bordered the large watering hole to take in the scene. The whole neighbourhood had turned out and the treetops were awash with colour. Hoopoes, cranes, kingfishers . . . even the vultures had shown up.

'They said there were going to be snacks, Sheila,' one grumpily muttered to his partner. 'I can't see a single bone to nibble on!'

'What's going on?' Linus whispered to Sheila.

'Beats me,' she chirped. 'Some kind of announcement, apparently.'

Down by the water's edge, there seemed to be a truce in the animal kingdom as everyone waited to see what the fuss was about.

7

There were lions, zebras, a pair of haughty-looking giraffes who appeared to think the whole thing was beneath them (which it kind of was, height-wise), a crocodile with a hungry smile, and next to him the local mayor, a quite pompous elephant, had shown up with his whole herd.

Suddenly, his loud trumpet brought the meeting to order. All the animals quietened down to hear what he had to say.

'Welcome, friends and, er, welcome, you animals who have tried to eat me, and also you animals that I try not to stand on,' began the mayor.

'That's us, Malcolm, he's talking about us!' a tiny meerkat said proudly to her husband.

'Thank you for gathering at such short notice. Our guest has travelled a great distance to be with us today. As your elected leader, I have granted him an audience. Let us hear what he has to say.' The elephant gestured with his trunk across the water.

All eyes turned to a lone albatross, normally unheard of in this part of the world, perched in the highest tree for miles around. On his leg he wore a band with three stripes that denoted he was a Flight Sergeant in the RBF.

'Thank you. I am Flight Sergeant Derek Pilchardton of the Royal Bird Force. I have a VERY important message to deliver.' His squawk was so loud it could be heard across the plains as he produced a parchment from around his neck, cleared his throat – 'Ahem' – and read with great self-importance:

From His Majesty's Animal Air Ministry:

Your Commonwealth needs you to join the fight against the enemy. We are asking all birds of flying age, the faster the better, to sign up and join the RBF.

Your mission will be to defend our shores, harass any invaders and help the human Royal Air Force defeat all enemy forces. You are to make your way to Britain as fast as the wind will take you. Godspeed.

Signed
Air Chief Marshal Sir Archibald Talon
Golden Eagle

The albatross rolled up the paper and tucked it back into his plumage.

'I shall be here for the rest of the day. Birds, please come and see me to sign up. Land animals, please be on a high state of alert. You will be called upon to do your duty very soon. '

The animals started muttering to one another, some excitedly and some less so. The lions and most of the elephants were looking very sceptical about helping any humans.

'This is it, sis!' said Linus, darting around impatiently. 'The chance I've been waiting for to prove how fast I am! Let's go!'

'Whoa, calm down, Linus! This isn't just about being able to fly fast. We would be going into battle, with humans who are bigger, nastier and more ruthless than us. Who have big machines – planes that could chew us up!'

'But, Ava, we can't sit around here and do nothing. You heard Flight Sergeant Pilchardton – they need all the birds they can get! And I'll finally get to fly with the falcons, in an elite RBF squadron!'

Ava groaned. 'Linus, you're a swift, maybe the fastest swift in all of Britain, Africa – maybe the world. Why are you so obsessed with the falcons?'

'Because they are the best, and I want to serve and fly with the best. So, don't you see, the better question would be: how can we NOT go?'

'But what have the humans ever done for us?' an old elephant trumpeted up at them grumpily. 'They hunt us for our meat, our skins, our tusks! And they steal our land! No good can come from this, or any other human war. Best keep out of it. Trust us elephants – we've seen it all before, and we never forget!'

The elephant had a point. As every animal knew, as far back as any species could remember, most humans were far too preoccupied with their own lives to notice anything of how the animal world helped them.

Only a rare few humans (kings and queens, presidents, prime ministers and a few high-ranking generals) were allowed to know that the animal world understood everything they said and did, and could communicate with them.

Over time, trust was earned and pacts were formed, and an uneasy alliance was formed between humans and animals.

So when a message needed to be sent from the animal to the human world or vice versa, a select squad of carrier pigeons would act as the secret go-between for the two kingdoms.

And if a human ever betrayed this alliance . . . Well, let's just say the same carrier pigeons would pursue the culprit for the rest of their lives, every minute of every day, and do what pigeons do

best . . . poo on their heads.

'Besides, Britain is so far away,' the old elephant continued. 'What does this war matter to us?'

'We were born in Britain! We migrated here for the winter last year, when we were no more than fledglings,' said Linus. He turned to his sister. 'Ava, you must remember the farm where we were born?'

'Of course, Linus. It was beautiful. We used to swoop around the farmyard and the skies above without a care in the world.'

'Exactly, and remember the young farmer and his family, who let us nest in their barn? Remember his children? A young brother and sister, just like us, who looked after us when we were fledglings learning to fly. The family waving at us as we swooped and soared above the fields, filling our beaks with as many bugs as we could eat. Birds and humans living side by side in harmony. If their freedom is in danger, then surely everyone else's is too, including the animal kingdom's. If we can do anything to help, then we have a duty to try.'

Ava nodded her head in resignation. She knew she was beaten, and there was no way she was going to let him go on his own.

'I can't believe I'm agreeing to this, but OK – on ONE

condition: you MUST listen to me. You're all I have in the world, little brother.'

'Thanks, sis. Come on, let's go!'

Signing their call-up papers with their beaks dipped in ink, they were instructed to report to Tangled Wood Airfield on the south coast of England in a week's time. 'Well done, you two,' Flight Sergeant Pilchardton said with a salute. 'Now, go and do your species proud!'

And with that, Linus and Ava soared away into the vast blue sky to prepare for their long journey, excited for the adventure that lay ahead and blissfully unaware of the grave danger they would be facing all too soon.

2

Linus and Ava flew away in the early hours the next morning, just before dawn. Below them they could see the lights of charcoal fires beginning to burn like beacons, as the first humans stirred and started their day. The swifts headed north, using the south-western flow of warm air to push them along. Even flying high, fast and hard, there wasn't a moment to lose. They would eat and sleep on the wing, and not land anywhere.

'We'll hug the west coast of Africa, like our parents and grandparents before us,' said Ava, 'then across the Mediterranean Sea and up over Spain and France. We should reach Tangled Wood Airfield in five days. Now, Linus, show me that speed you're famous for!'

Linus rolled over on to his back, stretched out, winked at his big sister and then dived into the clouds below.

'Show off,' Ava muttered fondly, and followed her younger brother into the steep dive.

They soared, banked and played in the clouds as they shook off the sleep of the night before. To the east they could see the sun start to rise over the plains, and the beautiful red earth below them began to reclaim its heat from the morning chill.

'What do you think our first mission will be?' Linus asked excitedly. 'I want to get right in the cockpit of the famous German

Messerschmitt 109 and make those pilots turn right around. I want to lead my own squadron of birds, with medals on my wing. I want to meet our animal Prime Minister, Sir Bertie Bulldog himself . . . and I want my own statue in Trafalgar Square!'

'You don't want much then?' his sister laughed. 'Linus, we're birds. Most humans have no idea we are coming to help, the enemy will be no pushover, their pilots and their planes will be tough to catch, let alone harass, and as for a statue! Good luck with that! The pigeons run Trafalgar Square; you'll have to impress them if that's what you want. Now, start by impressing *me* with less chatting and more flying!'

Gliding on the warm air, they picked up speed, and over the next couple of days they flew hard, skirting west Africa over the coast of

Nigeria, past Sierra Leone, then turning north over Senegal with the enormous Atlantic Ocean below, the huge waves breaking on the golden coast, until finally they were over Morocco and they could see the Mediterranean Sea ahead of them.

'We're making great progress,' Ava called to her brother. 'Two more days' hard flying and we'll be there!'

The birds were tired, but glancing below and seeing the Straits of Gibraltar spurred them on. They had finally reached Europe.

So far they hadn't seen many other birds, let alone any other animals. They were behind most of the swifts who had made the trip as part of their annual migration and who wanted to keep out of trouble, and they were too high and travelling too fast to see many other species of birds, but as they flew over southern Spain they hit an unexpected cloudy patch and had to go lower down to get their fill of insects for breakfast. As they descended, they spotted an Audouin's gull, a fisher bird common in this part of the world, its beak streaked with a familiar blood-red stain, and a squawk that could only come from a noisy, nosy seagull.

'*Brrrawwwkkk!*' the Spanish gull screeched, ascending from a dive in the ocean, a mouthful of sardines in his beak. 'Swifts? But only two of you, and travelling so fast? What's the hurry?'

Ava wasn't sure they should be telling a stranger their business, but before she could whisper this to her brother, he piped up.

'We've signed up to fight for the Allies. We're headed for the south of England. The sooner we get there, the sooner we can see some action!'

Ava groaned inwardly, but the stranger seemed to warm to the birds.

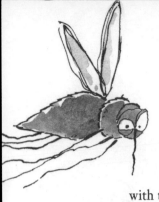

'Hey, good for you. But, my young friends, you must be careful. Today you have the good fortune to meet an ally, but not all animals are sympathetic to our cause. The wasps and the mosquitos have already sided with the enemy.'

'So it's true,' Ava sighed.

There had been rumours around the watering hole that some animals might see siding with the enemy as an opportunity to get rid of some of their competitors and move up the pecking order of the animal kingdom, rather than uniting to fight for the freedom of humans and animals alike. Wasps had always had an attitude problem and were angry ALL THE TIME, and as for mosquitos, they were either biting you or you were eating them . . . which didn't make for great relations.

'Alas, yes,' the gull answered. 'But it's not just them. I've heard of birds, mammals, even sea creatures siding with the enemy to get a leg-up – or a fin-up.'

In other words, for all her brother's bravado, they needed to be careful.

'Ah, I wish I was a little younger,' the gull continued. 'I'd love to show those thugs a thing or two.

I see the dreaded U-boats off the coast

all the time and aim my droppings on the

captain's head when they surface. Scored a

direct hit last week. So much fun – the fool

was covered in it.

But I'm just one bird, and a simple fisher bird at that; what can I do! Speaking of which, would you care for some breakfast?' He offered up a severed sardine head.

'Err, no, we're good, thanks,' Linus said, as he snatched a passing insect out of the air and gobbled it down.

'Urgh, insects,' winced the seagull. He greedily finished the last of the silvery fish. 'I also heard from my cousin in Galicia that France has fallen and Britain will be next! Despite the best efforts of the Allies, they were pushed back to Dunkirk. Over three hundred thousand men made it out, but scores perished, alongside many seabirds shot out of the sky, and countless seals who tried to clear the mines. I don't normally care for seals, too greedy, but you have to say those are some brave mammals . . .' He trailed off. 'Anyway, Godspeed, and may La Virgen del Carmen be with you.'

The swifts looked at him blankly.

'The patron saint of fishermen! You swifts, so fast, but you know nothing!' He winked and went into a steep dive down to the shining sea in search of more sardines.

'We need to be careful,' Ava said to her brother. 'Now we've reached Europe we'll see more animals involved in the war and we won't know which side they're on. Until we get to England, if anyone asks us, let's just say we're migrating on our own as it's faster that way.'

Linus nodded. He'd been carried away with the adventure of it all and hadn't really thought about actually being in danger. Hearing the gull talking about birds falling out of the sky . . . For the first time in his life, he felt a tiny bit scared.

'Come on, Linus, we're expected at Tangled Wood for our first briefing in two days. We need to push on.'

The siblings pinned back their wings and sped off, eager to get to the safety of Tangled Wood Airfield as quickly as possible – not realising that where they were heading was one of the most dangerous places on earth for human or bird.

3

For two more days and nights the swifts flew high and fast, until they saw the north coast of France, and beyond that the English Channel and the white cliffs of Dover, shimmering in the far distance.

'We're almost there!' Linus said with relief. 'I'm going to eat so many tasty English hoverflies and have a good sleep tonight! Then I'll be ready for action!'

Exhausted, the small birds were keen to find Tangled Wood, their new home, but just as they were about to start to cross the Channel and make for the white cliffs, Ava called to her brother.

'Linus, down there to the right!' Ava had spotted two planes weaving sharply in and out of the clouds. A German Messerschmitt 109, with its distinctive yellow nose, and a British Hurricane were

locked in a dogfight, a beautiful but deadly dance.

The birds could hear the *rat-tat-tat* of machine guns and it was clear even from eight hundred feet away that the Hurricane was in trouble. It was desperately making for the safety of home, but the German pilot was right on its tail.

Without missing a beat, Linus dived through the clouds.

'Linus, wait! What did I say? DON'T GO ON YOUR OWN!' Ava took off after him.

Breaking through the clouds, the small bird levelled off his shallow dive right behind the German plane. The pilot had the Hurricane in his sights and was moving in for the kill. Instinctively, Linus pinned back his wings, picked up speed and moved in front of the cockpit of the Messerschmitt, into the pilot's line of vision. Not entirely sure what he was seeing, or how a bird could fly so fast, the surprised German airman tried rolling the plane to shake the pest, but to no avail; Linus stuck to the front of the plane.

In the cockpit of the Hurricane just ahead, Flight Lieutenant Ginger Thomas of 505 Squadron was in deep trouble: out of ammunition and almost out of fuel. It had all started so well. They had moved to attack a group of German fighters over the Channel. He'd downed one, and a probable second, but in the chaos he'd been separated from his squadron and was now being tailed by this Messerschmitt.

Ginger knew that any second his trusty but inferior Mark 1 Hurricane was about to be peppered by the powerful cannon of the German aircraft. He didn't fancy bailing out. If he could just make it across the Dover Strait to the British coastline, he knew the fighter behind him wouldn't have too much fuel left and would have to head for home and not risk a foray over enemy territory. But that was a big 'if'. Right now, as he looked in his cockpit mirror, all he could see was a small brown speck buzzing around the enemy's cockpit, like an annoying wasp after a jam sandwich.

What the dickens is that? the young pilot thought to himself. He didn't have time to stick around. Whatever it was, it was distracting the pursuing German, which meant he had a chance of making it home!

The German pilot was getting exasperated. And just a little annoyed! His quarry was escaping and it was all down to this crazy bird in front of him! He was running out of fuel and pretty soon he'd have to turn back for the safety of his airfield in France. In desperation, he threw back his canopy and tried to shoo the bird away. Drawing level to it, he swatted his hand in the direction of the bird and just managed to knock it off course, sending it spiralling through the air. Just as he did, a second bird flew in from nowhere and clawed at his face, flapping around the cockpit.

He was now losing his bearings. Bewildered, he looked up to see that he was now perilously close to the sea cliff, and it was too late to pull out. All he could do was to crash-land into the ocean. *How has this happened?* the German thought to himself. *Why are these crazy birds attacking me!*

Ginger simply couldn't believe what had just happened. One minute he was done for, the next he saw the German plane ditch in to the English Channel. Thank goodness! The enemy must have run out of fuel

. . . but what on earth was that brown speck? A bird? It couldn't be! It looked like it was deliberately attacking the plane! As he saw the pilot exit from the canopy and get into his life raft, he felt conflicted. He hated the enemy and wanted to rid the skies of them, but now the German had been downed, he became a human. He was a young man, just like him. He shook himself free of the thought and, feeling lucky and grateful, headed for the safety of home.

'Ava! AVA!' Linus circled as low as he could, calling his sister's name for all he was worth.

After he'd recovered from being swatted, he'd righted himself and looked back to see Ava disappear into the cockpit. A second later, he'd watched in horror as the unthinkable had occurred and the plane had crash landed, with a gentle flop, into the sea.

He had seen the German pilot get out into his life raft, before the plane had slowly and agonisingly sunk beneath the lapping waves. Ava was nowhere to be seen.

As dusk gave way to darkness, he circled for hours, his wings aching with the effort, growing weaker and weaker as the minutes passed. There was still no sign of Ava. *What have I done?* he thought to himself. *My stupid bravado. I've lost her, and it's all my fault!*

Finally, feeling exhausted, miserable and alone, he was about to turn to fly inland, when he heard a low, ominous drone and looked up to see a squadron of mechanical beasts fly over him.

'German bombers,' he whispered in fear and awe. Finding shelter beneath the cliff's edge, he counted five or six huge Dorniers passing overhead. The noise was incredible, and he had to admit he felt more than a little afraid, and helpless for whoever the bombing raid was destined for.

As the noise grew more distant, he was filled with despair. How would he, a tiny swift, be able to fight against such airpower? Maybe signing up had been a huge mistake. He watched them disappear into the distance.

About to turn away, something caught his eye. At the front of the squadron, silhouetted against the setting sun, he could see a bird flapping away. His heart soared. Was it Ava? Had she made it?

He strained his eyes to see. No. The bird was far too big to be his sister, and rather than harassing or attacking the leading plane, it looked like the bird was flying alongside, almost guiding it to its target.

He shook his head. He was exhausted, physically and mentally. He must be imagining things. For a moment, he had no idea what he should do next . . . what would Ava want him to do? He shut his eyes and pictured her face. Keep calm and carry on, that's what she'd say. If she was out there somewhere, the best place for her to find him would be Tangled Wood. He puffed up his chest, spread his wings and slowly made towards his new home, his heart heavy with anguish for his missing sister.

Fighter Group 11 of the Royal Bird Force was stationed at Tangled Wood, a disused farm three miles inland from Dover on the south coast.

The firepit still burning was the only sign of life as Linus landed in the middle of the farmyard. Feeling utterly dejected, he looked around, unsure where to go or who to report to. Hearing noises coming from the nearest barn, he made his way to the slightly ajar barn door.

Inside he heard singing and laughing, and, as he got closer, the sound of a small accordion. He peered in to see a barn full of peregrine falcons, with their famous yellow beaks and claws, speckled breasts and beautiful grey wings. The various stripes of light and dark blues and white in the rings around their legs signalled their different ranks. Linus took a breath. They looked every bit like the elite of the RBF he had imagined. He wished Ava could see this and, as much as his heart panged for his sister, he knew this was where he belonged. A small group of field mice played the accordion, jumping on it in perfect time, and plates of seed and chopped-up meat were being served by a team of dutiful-looking shrews. It was clear they were celebrating something.

'Ladies and gentlemen, avians and mammals . . .'

The music faded as a handsome-looking peregrine falcon hopped up on a stool to address the barn.

'Today A-Squadron scored our biggest victory so far. We harassed three planes with a combination of teamwork, talons and, as always . . . poo! In poo we trust!' He laughed.

A massive squawk went up in the barn. The falcon smiled and continued.

'As we harassed them out of the sky, they were so confused and, in some cases, blinded by poo, they were easy pickings for our human boys in the RAF. This is down to our incredible speed – no one can beat the speed of a falcon.

We heroes of A-Squadron are well on our way to becoming legendary, so tonight, we celebrate!'

A roar of approval went up, and the music was about to kick in again when Linus piped up. 'Ex-excuse me . . . Sorry to interrupt, and well done on your battle today. I'm Linus. I'm here to volunteer for the RBF. Am I in the right place?'

'Err, I don't think so,' another falcon who was stood to the side of the leader answered sarcastically. 'Are you a peregrine falcon? *Well?*'

'Well, no, I'm a swift . . . obviously,' Linus answered, a little confused.

'Exactly, a swift!' he scoffed. 'Well, Mr Swift, this squadron, A-Squadron, is made up exclusively of falcons. And not just any falcons – peregrine falcons. We are the fittest, the fastest and the most ferocious. This here is Squadron Leader Marcus Falco, the fastest falcon there is.' He gestured to the falcon standing on the chair, who smiled indulgently at his friend, clearly enjoying the attention. 'And I am his wingman, Marmaduke. Only I get to fly by his side, and only *falcons* get to fly with *us*.'

'But I'm here to join the best,' Linus protested. 'I'm the fastest there is!'

'Are you stupid?' Marmaduke shouted as he hopped menacingly towards the small bird. 'I said you aren't needed, so why don't you just shove off?'

'But I've flown all the way from Africa with my sister to fight with you!' Linus couldn't believe what was happening. Had he lost Ava for nothing?

'And you can jolly well fly back with your sister. If you are anything to go by she'll be stupid and cloth-eared too.'

Something inside Linus snapped. Falcon or no falcon, no one talked about Ava like that!

'My sister is as brave as any bird here, and I'd bet she's twice the flyer you'll ever be, you bully.'

Marmaduke puffed up his feathers and loomed over Linus, his sharp talons twitching. 'Stand back, falcons – time this little *birdbrain* got taught a lesson.'

Marmaduke took flight and launched himself at Linus, but the swift was too fast and flew out of the way, making the larger bird miss and crash upside down into a pile of straw bales.

The barn was shocked into silence, all the birds with their beaks wide open (although Linus could have sworn he saw a couple of field mice looking at each other and trying hard not to laugh) –

silence, apart from Linus's heart drumming loudly in his chest. What had he done? He'd only just got here and he'd made an enemy straight away.

'Why, you little upstart, I'm going to rip your innards out!' the humiliated falcon screeched as he emerged covered in straw and looking more than a little silly.

Linus made to dodge out of the way again, but before he could, the barn door creaked open noisily.

'Now now, Mr Marmaduke – don't go getting your feathers in a twist.' A huge speckled goshawk with piercing red eyes leaned up against the barn door. It was clear he wasn't the least bit intimidated by the falcons. Linus couldn't help but be very impressed. The goshawk continued to address the barn in a deep, slow country drawl.

'I think this young 'un might have strayed into the wrong barn is all. No need for those talons to come out!' The blue and white stripes of the ring attached to his leg told Linus that he carried the rank of Squadron Leader, just like Marcus Falco.

'Keep out of this, Atticus!' the enraged falcon replied uncertainly. 'This is between me and the swift.'

'Ah, that, young man, is where you are wrong,' he chuckled. He addressed the swift. 'Linus, isn't it?'

'Yes,' said the swift, unsure what on earth was going on.

How did this old goshawk know his name, and why was he sticking up for him? He was certainly glad that he was; he didn't fancy his chances against a room full of falcons!

The older bird continued in a breezy manner, almost oblivious to the glare of the furious falcon.

'Well, you're in the right place, just the wrong barn. This is A-Squadron. You're with me in B-Squadron, just opposite. The name's Atticus and I'm your Squadron Leader. I've been waiting for you. Now, come along, we've got an early start tomorrow!' he added breezily.

More than grateful, Linus made to move, but the angry falcon blocked his path.

'Marmaduke!' The older goshawk smiled as he moved to protect the small swift. 'I don't need to remind you that I outrank you, and even if we discount rank for a minute, which I am more than happy to, if this young swift is part of my squadron, do you really think that I won't protect him, and do you *really* want to pick a fight with a very relaxed, but increasingly annoyed goshawk?' He very subtly spread his talons as the peregrine's eyes widened. Realising he was beaten, the falcon gave way and let Linus pass.

'I'll see you in the air tomorrow, *swift*,' he whispered menacingly as Linus flew past. Marmaduke tried to save face. 'Come on then, falcons, let's get on with the party and let B-Squadron get their *beauty sleep*. They'll need all the rest they can get to keep up with us. Music!'

The mice struck up on the accordion and the party went back to full swing as Linus and the goshawk made their way outside.

'Well, you know how to make an entrance, Master Linus,' the goshawk chuckled as they made their way across the farmyard.

'Gosh, I'm sorry! I didn't mean to offend anyone, least of all the falcons.'

'Oh, don't you be worrying about that, and certainly don't concern yourself with Marmaduke – he needs bringing down a

peg or two; like so many young birds nowadays he's got more speed than sense! Now, here is your new home.' He opened the door on to a cosy barn illuminated by candlelight with small nests dotted along the first floor and the eaves of the roof. The sound of light snoring was oddly comforting.

'There's your billet up there,' he said, pointing his wing to a small nest in the eaves. 'You get a good night's sleep and I'll introduce you to the squadron tomorrow. Oh, one last thing – my friend Derek the albatross said there'd be two of you?'

Linus's heart plummeted. He didn't want to say it out loud. It would make it real. 'My sister, Ava,' he whispered. 'I lost her near the cliffs. She's missing in action.'

'Ah . . .' The old hawk nodded to himself sadly. 'I'm sorry to hear that. Happens all too often. Try and put it out of your mind tonight. She could still turn up! Now, you get some rest, good night.'

Linus crawled into his tiny nest, racked all over again with worry for his sister. The warm hay smell and the sleepy snuffles of other animals around the barn only made him feel more alone than ever.

'Ava,' he whispered to himself in the dark. 'I'm so sorry. You only signed up to keep me safe, and look what I've done. I'm not

sure I can do this without you. I'll find you, I promise I will!'

Trying not to cry, his head hit the soft mossy twigs in his nest and he succumbed to a deep, dreamless sleep.

4

'*Cock a doodle dooooo!* Rise and shine, you lovely lot! *Cock a doodle dooo!* Roll call in five minutes!'

Linus prised one eye open to see pale light trickling in through the barn doors. An old cockerel was sounding the wake-up call, breaking the silence of the dawn, and another bird was lighting a candle, casting a warm glow on the sleeping shapes around him. Linus hadn't slept in a nest for so long that he'd forgotten what a good night's sleep felt like. He looked around his new home for the first time. Dotted around the top two floors of the barn were small nests of all shapes and sizes, from which an array of different birds were slowly emerging, ruffling their feathers and hopping down to the floor where a group of busy-looking mice were filling several birdbaths. The nests were all full, bar one to Linus's right, and he glanced over to see an empty space where Ava should be.

He felt a dull ache in his stomach. All he could think about was his sister.

He was racked with worry, but he had to try to put it out of his head.

She'd want you to fly. Get out there today and show them what you can do!

'Ah, young Master Linus!' The booming screech of the goshawk echoed across the barn. 'I trust you slept well. You certainly sounded like you did with all your snoring.'

The rest of the birds in the barn cackled good-naturedly.

'Can I impose on you to hop down here and meet your new B-Squadron mates?'

Linus hopped down and was immediately surrounded by five birds, who dwarfed him.

'So this is the speedster you've promised will whip us into shape!' a friendly magpie piped up.

'This here is Pica,' Atticus gestured to the magpie, who held out a wing. 'Not the fastest in the squadron, but definitely the most intelligent.' Pica beamed at the compliment. 'She has her ear to the ground, keeps in contact with D-Squadron, the bats who act as our radar department, normally nocturnal, but with the war on

they've been working round the clock. Plus, she works with the underground mole network, the very brave volunteers who keep tabs on enemy activity. She's also our best scrounger, so if you want anything – your favourite insects, more straw for your nest – just let her know.'

Pica winked at Linus and clicked her beak.

'One last thing,' Atticus went on. 'She steals anything not nailed down, so watch out. I'm just glad she's on our side.'

'What can I say? It's in my nature!' shrugged the magpie.

'These two over here,' continued Atticus, 'are our twins Victor and Vera, local marsh harriers. They're deadly quick and they know every inch of the marshes around the coastline. Any questions, you ask them – plus they are good at catching breakfast.' The two birds shook Linus by the wing.

'And the last of the motley crew who make up this squadron of misfits is still asleep. Tyyyyrone! You lazy so-and-so! Get uupppp!' Atticus yelled.

The moon-like round face of a barn owl poked his head out of a nest on the top floor. 'Oh. Hello. Nice to make your acquaintance,' he said, blinking in the daylight. 'For the record, I'm not lazy, I'm nocturnal, so . . . I'm going back to bed!' He yawned. With that he

disappeared back into his nest.

Atticus shook his head in resignation. 'There's no finer flyer and hunter at night, but he does need his beauty sleep.' He sighed. 'So, Linus, that's our B-Squadron and your new family. Now, come on outside for roll call and I'll explain to you how we work. But before I forget, let me just give you this.' He smiled as he clipped a light-and dark-blue ring on to Linus's tiny leg.

'Good to have you flying with us, Pilot Officer Linus the Swift.'

The goshawk and the rest of the squadron saluted. Linus saluted back, his heart swelling with pride.

They were a raggle-taggle crew of all shape and sizes, and a world away from the smartly preened falcons, but they seemed friendly and right now Linus could do with all the friends he could get.

The cockerel finished his squawking as the birds made their way into the farmyard, where they all fell to their respective squadrons. Linus looked up to see an old clock on the top of the barn below a rusty weather vane. Even though it was 6 a.m., the farmyard was alive with activity.

All around them an army of field mice and voles were preparing breakfast, filling troughs full of seeds and grains.

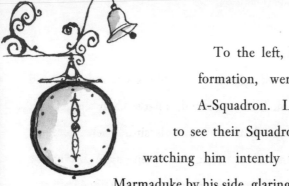

To the left, standing in perfect formation, were the falcons of A-Squadron. Linus looked over to see their Squadron Leader, Marcus, watching him intently with his wingman Marmaduke by his side, glaring at the little swift.

A squadron of pigeons of all colours and sizes *coo-cooed* about, pecking at seeds on the floor, and Linus could see D-Squadron – the radar bats – hanging upside down under a shaded sloped roof that extended from one of the barn doors.

At the front of the farmyard, the door of the house opened and a busy-looking buzzard, flanked by six officious-looking starlings, hopped confidently towards the farmyard to address the troops.

'That's Wing Commander Butler,' whispered Atticus. 'He's in charge of all the squadrons in Flight Group II. He's a good sort, though always stressed, and don't let him anywhere near a rabbit, even in wartime . . . Buzzards and rabbits can get very messy, if you know what I mean.'

The old hawk grimaced.

'So,' he continued, 'here's how it all works. Six o'clock sharp every morning, on the parade ground. That's when we get our orders for the day ahead. Our mission is simple: to intercept, harass, sabotage and, where possible, destroy enemy planes by any means, "be they beak, claw or poo . . . in poo we trust!". That's the RBF mantra,' he chuckled. 'We are the first line of defence of the country, and we work alongside the humans. Their airfield is just the other side of the hedgerow. Not that they even know we're here, thankfully.

'Now, thanks to our bats in D-Squadron, who, as I said, act as our radar, we know when enemy planes are coming before the humans do. As soon the bats hear them inbound, they pass the flight path to C-Squadron – that's our carrier pigeons – and they take the messages to the human squadrons. Then the falcons of A-Squadron fly to intercept the enemy and attack their planes before the humans get there.'

'Sounds amazing!' Linus had to admit, he was excited, and this was it, his first day on the front line, even with Ava's loss weighing so heavily, he couldn't wait to get started and avenge his sister. 'So what's *our* job?' the little swift asked excitedly.

'Well, we, er, perform more of a support role really, spotting aircraft, wasps, helping guard animals working in defences . . .'

'What?' Linus was confused.

'Err, yes, His Majesty's Animal Air Ministry in London decided that the peregrines were to be given the task of leading the missions, and B-Squadron would fly support. It's a bit who you know, not what you know, if you get my drift!' Atticus answered, looking embarrassed.

Linus was crestfallen. He had come all this way to fly with the best. The falcons! He'd done his bit and signed up, and he knew he was as fast as any of these birds – faster, even! And now he was going to spend the war guarding defences, and spotting wasps or suspicious-looking animals!

They should have never left Africa, and his sister had been lost in vain.

'Good morning, my brave avians and mammals of the RBF!' Wing Commander Butler piped up. 'Today we have *beaucoup de* movement. Our underground mole network heard last night from the humans that there are bombing raids expected all over the south of England. Also last night, somehow the blackout blinds were stolen, and the clock tower lights were turned on at the town hall.'

'That's a worry,' Atticus whispered to Linus. 'There's a rumour there's a traitor hereabouts. Some say local foxes, but others think it's closer to home. The odd thing is, only we and the other two fighter groups stationed nearby have the keys to that clock tower, because we use it as an observation post. So either there was a break-in or the traitor is among us!'

'The whole place was clobbered,' the Wing Commander continued. 'I've spoken to the Animal Air Ministry in London and to our other fighter groups of 10 and 12 and we are on high alert. Bats, I know you've been working around the clock but we need D-Squadron to get to the cliffs as soon as possible.'

The chief bat saluted its webbed wing and the colony of bats took flight to head for the nearby sea cliffs to begin their watch.

Butler continued. 'Pigeons, I need C-Squadron to get to the airfield. Make sure you are ready with your backpacks for your messages, as you're in for a very busy day.'

A brown and grey wood pigeon, their Squadron Leader, gave a coo and a nod (although as far as Linus could see, they nodded all the time), and the squadron waddled off in the direction of a nearby field accompanied by their ground crew, a small army of rodents carrying their backpacks, and a wagon of seed.

'A-Squadron! Falcons, the Animal Air Ministry has asked me to commend you for your efforts yesterday, although they seem convinced that you helped down FOUR enemy aircraft, not the three that were claimed. There was a report of a German Messerschmitt that went down off the coast last night, brought down by two birds.'

'That was us!' Linus exclaimed. 'Me and my sister! We did that.' Before he could say anything more, Marcus piped up over him. 'Yes, thank you, my second-in-command has just informed me that was us. It must have happened on his last patrol of the evening.'

'Well, better make it four confirmed downed enemy aircraft then. Congratulations, you're getting quite a name for yourselves. We are all expecting more of the same today. Dismissed.'

Marmaduke beamed smugly, looking very pleased with himself.

Linus was furious. 'But that's not true, we downed that plane!' he shouted, breaking ranks.

The shocked Wing Commander turned to face the tiny bird.

'I believe you meant to say, *That's not true, SIR*,' he said in a low, commanding tone. He directed his gaze at Atticus as if to demand an explanation.

'Uh, Linus the swift, sir,' Atticus explained as he introduced the new recruit. 'Joined us last night. Proper speedster he is, just what B-Squadron needs to become a front-line fighting force, if we're just given the chance. He's a bit spirited, is all. We'll work on that.'

'Well, Master Linus, welcome to Fighter Group 11. I'm sure you've made *quite* the impression already,' he said, glancing over at the falcons, who stared back at Linus with contempt.

Linus knew he was running the risk of getting into trouble, but he didn't care. Ava had downed that plane. Her reputation was worth fighting for.

The Wing Commander held Linus's gaze for a moment then turned to Atticus.

'Now, sorry, old thing, but you know the orders from the Air Ministry. Peregrines do the fighting – they are the fastest we have. Plus, you know they are the most connected, friends in high places and all that. Anyway, I need you and your birds over at Romney Marsh. Some of our nests got clobbered on that raid last night, so I need you to fly protection for the ground crew rebuilding it.

There are rumours of thousands of wasps around the marsh and – I can't believe I'm saying this – the moles think a rogue bird guided the enemy in last night. Our own kind, working against us! I never thought I'd see the day.' He shook his head sadly. 'So be watchful, be careful. Dismissed!' He gave Linus one last glance, and for just a split second the young swift was sure he could see the tiniest crack of a smile. Then the Wing Commander turned and flew back to the farmhouse, barking orders, followed closely by his team of self-important starlings.

'Best we get going.' Atticus turned to usher the swift away, but winced as a whistle came from behind them.

'Swift!' It was Marcus, the Squadron Leader of the falcons. 'What on earth do you think gives you the right to steal our victories? Marmaduke himself told me he forgot to chalk up that extra plane last night after he came in late, and here you are trying to claim it for your own. You should be ashamed of yourself!'

'But I swear it WAS me! Well, it was my sister really; she was the proper hero.'

'I see, and where is she now? Hmm?'

'She's missing, sir. She went down with the plane.'

Marcus scoffed. 'A likely story! A tiny swift taking down a

Messerschmitt? Come on, now.' He leaned down to Linus. 'Listen here. I mean you no harm, but we are the best fighting group in the whole RBF because everyone knows their place, from the pigeons and the bats to the elite peregrines. So what say you let us natural-born flyers concentrate on the combat and you do your best to support us, OK?' The peregrine nodded to Atticus and then took off to catch up with his squadron.

'Come on, Linus. We might not be deemed worthy to be on the front line, but we can still do some good. Let's get you up in the air where you belong; you'll feel much better.' He placed a reassuring wing around the young swift's shoulder, and they took off together on his first mission.

5

Atticus was right. As soon as Linus was up in the air, he felt like he was home again. The young swift played with the currents as his leader explained their roles and the mission ahead.

'Linus, you are by far the fastest so I need you at the head of the squadron. You'll be the first to see any danger and report it to me. DO NOT take matters into your own hands, and never attack without a wingman. That is THE most important rule when you fly with the RBF. I'll be at the centre of the wing calling the shots, leaving the twins at either side and Pica and Tyrone bringing up the rear.'

'Right, but where is Tyrone?' The swift looked around for the owl but he was nowhere to be seen.

'Well, he'll be along later when it gets dark. He keeps his eye

on the ground and on anything attacking us from behind,' Atticus said.

'And I keep my eye out for any scavenging opportunities,' Pica cackled.

'Er, not officially,' the hawk answered awkwardly.

'I didn't hear you complain when I brought you those sausages I stole from the butcher's last week!' With that the whole squadron fell about laughing.

Linus was beginning to feel a bit better. His squadron seemed to be the misfits of the whole RBF, and it certainly wasn't what he thought flying in the bird force would be, but they'd welcomed him as one of their own and at least he was up in the air. He was flying! And he was certain, if he was just given the opportunity, the whole fighter group, even the peregrines, would see what a great flyer he was. He pinned his wings back and sped through the clouds towards Romney Marsh.

The marshes, a patchwork of wetlands and waterways on the south coast of England between Kent and East Sussex, were famed for being a haven for smugglers known as 'Owlers'. They were so named because the local owl population, like Tyrone and his parents and grandparents before him, had worked as lookouts for

them. The water voles and stoats still made a roaring trade smuggling everything from wool to grain. The place had a sense of mystery about it, but it was also very valuable to the army. The nearby Royal Military Canal was being heavily fortified. If the Germans were going to invade, it might be here, which meant that the RBF had a big responsibility to guard the area.

The bombing raid that had taken place the night before had put the local RAF airfield out of action, plus a small outhouse barn where a vitally important squadron of bats had been stationed. As the squadron touched down, a local hedgehog with a small team of field mice were doing their best to clear the rubble and repair some of the beams for the bats to be able to hang.

'Good day to you, Mrs Erin!' said Atticus as he landed.

'Atti! Thank goodness you're here! I've got my best mice working around the clock. This barn has to be up and running or the bats will have nowhere to hang, which means a good five-mile stretch of the coast without their radar. We've had two wasp raids already today, and my poor master carpenter has been stung twice on the bottom.'

A mouse grimaced as he presented his raw bum to the hawk by way of evidence.

Atticus blushed. 'Right, yes, er, well, my birds are raring to go, so you just keep calm and carry on and leave the rest to us.'

He turned to the squad. 'Twins, I need you low over the marshes. Look out for any low-flying insects and wasps. And remember, DON'T eat any mice – there's a truce while the war's on. And I can't have a major diplomatic incident.'

'Ugh,' the marsh harriers grumbled, then saluted as they took off. 'I was looking forward to a bit of potted vole,' Vera moaned.

Atticus shook his head. 'Pica, you stay close to the ground and keep your eyes open . . . and don't steal anything.'

'FINE,' the magpie answered begrudgingly, her wings crossed behind her back.

'Which means you and I, Linus, take to the skies. Shall we?'

With that the old goshawk launched himself into the air, gaining altitude quickly. Linus could see he was a gifted flyer, and pretty soon they were a thousand or so feet up, looking down on the shimmering sea meeting the coastline.

'I had no idea you were that fast, Squadron Leader!'

'Well, I'm better in forests – my natural habitat, you see – but I can still turn on the speed in the air when I want to. Now, let's see YOUR speed, little swift.'

For the next few hours the two birds patrolled up and down the coastline.

They saw small fishing boats on the water and the local gulls following them for scraps, and once they observed a pair of Hurricanes fly a few thousand feet above them on a patrol, but they saw no German planes, wasps or any suspicious-looking birds.

The twins, Victor and Vera, flew up a couple of hours in to report that they'd had a skirmish with a small group of wasps,

but that they'd been despatched and were now being enjoyed by a grateful local spider.

About an hour before dusk Atticus decided to call it a day.

'I think Mrs Erin should be about done with the repairs now. Time to head for home, Linus. Sorry you didn't see any action on your first sortie, but that's no bad thing – better to ease yourself in. Linus . . . ?'

The small bird was too distracted to answer. He was looking down on a small V-formation a thousand feet below him, making with great speed for the airfield. He could see they were carrying something, but couldn't make out what. Whatever it was, he sensed they were up to no good.

'Squadron Leader, group of unidentified birds heading towards the airfield. I'm going to investigate.'

Before Atticus could answer, Linus headed into a steep dive that his leader couldn't hope to keep up with.

'No, Linus! Pull up! I said never attack without a wingman. WAIT!' screamed the goshawk, but it was too late.

As he sped through the air and made up the ground between him and the V-shaped column, Linus could see that they were some kind of geese, each carrying a basket of rubble and destined for the bats' outhouse!

They're starting a bombing run! he thought to himself. He turned to see where Atticus was and realised he was too far behind. Linus had to act now.

He sped up and with all his effort he flew to the back of the column and started pecking at the harnesses of the baskets the geese were using to store their rubble bombs.

'*Brawwkkkk!* What are you doing, you fool?' a goose squawked as his basket of rubble came loose and tumbled down into the sea.

'My duty, you traitor!' Linus screamed in reply, as he went on to the next bird.

The geese began to panic and fly out of formation. One by one they collided with each other or panicked and spilled their deadly loads of rubble harmlessly on to the marshes.

Linus was ecstatic. It was only his first day and already he'd foiled an enemy mission. They'd give him a medal for this, and the peregrines would respect him for sure.

One tiny thing was bothering him though. The geese weren't going anywhere – they were just circling around, looking furious. Why weren't they scared stiff or trying to get away?

Atticus arrived at the scene and Linus flew towards him proudly.

'Don't worry, boss, all under control. I spotted these traitors

about to begin a bombing run against our own. You can round them up now.'

Pica, Tyrone and the twins finally arrived at the scene and looked on in horror. Which was not the reaction Linus was hoping for. 'Boss, guys, capture them . . . Right?'

Atticus flew over to the lead goose. 'Pierre, I'm so sorry. Are you and your squadron OK? It's his first day, and he's VERY headstrong and very fast. He took off through the clouds before I could stop him.'

'*Pierre?* You *know* this bird?' Linus asked his Squadron Leader in disbelief, a slow sinking sensation taking hold of him.

'Linus, allow me to introduce you to Wing Commander Pierre Boucher, of the Canadian Geese Squadron.'

'*He's on our side,*' Linus whispered in horror to himself.

'He's on our side,' Atticus calmly repeated. 'He was on the way with his squadron to help REBUILD the airfield.'

'Oh, my . . . I'm so sorry, sir,' said Linus, hanging his head in shame.

'You are a very fast flyer, my little swift, and very brave,' Pierre said. 'It's a shame your brains seem to be in your wings. Geese, *ALLEZ!*'

With that the geese followed their leader in a perfect wing formation to look for the rubble that had been dropped.

'We'd better go and help them, hadn't we, Linus?' the old goshawk said sternly.

Linus said nothing. The squadron looked at him with a mixture of sympathy and disappointment, but nothing could make him feel worse than he already did. It had been his first mission and he'd let down his squadron, his species and the whole war effort. Maybe those elephants back in Africa were right. This was not his fight at all.

6

Wing Commander Butler, however, wasn't as forgiving.

'You FOOL! Do you have any idea what you've done? This could be a MAJOR international incident. The animal Prime Minister Sir Bertie Bulldog himself is already on the phone to his Canadian counterpart, who is demanding to know why any Canadian animals should help with the war effort if this is how they will be treated! And why? Because one little swift wanted to prove he could mix with the big birds. Maybe those falcons were right after all.'

Linus went to answer, but Atticus held him back by his wing.

'You should feel lucky I'm not transferring you out of the group,' he continued, 'and don't think I wouldn't if we weren't so short-winged. Dismissed!' he bellowed. He turned to study a map on the wall, and began being briefed by a group of blue tits, leaving Atticus and Linus to hop out of the farmhouse HQ with their tails between their wings.

'Well, that's it. I've blown it!' said Linus miserably, as they flew back to their barn.

'Now now, my young friend. Don't beat yourself up – anyone could have made that mistake.'

'Did you ever make that mistake?'

'Well, no, good point, but I can't fly as fast as you, remember, so I have more time to think. Get your head down for a rest and the world will look like a different place tomorrow, I promise you.'

The little bird flew up to his nest and pondered his future. Among his family, his community, he was the fastest swift in a generation. But here that didn't count for much at all. If only Ava was here to give him some advice.

He felt like a failure, and he had no idea how to put it right.

*

It wasn't the sun creeping in through the dusty barn that woke Linus next morning but the weird smell, and then, as he opened his eyes, the frankly terrifying sight of a poor dead creature on a plate ready for his breakfast that confronted him.

'Argh! What is that?! And what time is it?' he asked blearily.

'First light, and it's a newt, of course,' said Atticus, perched on a nearby beam. 'My favourite meal at breakfast. Good brain-food! Especially as we can't catch mice at the moment – they're vital to the war effort, you see. Right, boys?' He waved at a pair of mice, who were part of the ground crew; they looked at each other nervously, smiled at the goshawk, then slowly backed away towards the safety of the barn door.

'Now, eat up! We've got work to do.'

Linus looked around.

The whole squadron was still fast asleep, the only noise coming from Tyrone the owl, who was snoring his head off as usual.

'Er, newts aren't really my thing . . . Sorry,' said Linus. 'I'm more of an insect guy. I mean, look at my beak, it's tiny!'

'Hmm, no pleasing some people. Newts made me what I am today! Well, you'll have to find some insects on the way then. Should be plenty.'

'Where are we going?' Linus asked, stretching his wings.

'To prove those naysayers wrong. You are fast, Linus, I saw that yesterday. The fastest I've ever seen, I'll wager, but you need discipline and training. That's where I come in! Let's go.'

Linus wasn't quite sure what to think. After the embarrassment he'd caused his squadron last night, he'd do anything to make amends. But he knew he could fly, fast. What could the old goshawk teach him that he didn't already know?

Atticus ushered the small swift out of the barn and up into the sky.

'Linus, listen to me,' he said as they flew up over the coast. 'You are faster than any of those peregrines. I think you could be the finest flier in the RBF – but you have much to learn. Watching you last night, you were far too headstrong and as you sped away I noticed one important thing. You didn't even give yourself time to pull out of the dive. You're obsessed with peregrine falcons, but that's the one thing you swifts have over them. They are so fast in a dive, but they over-commit; they can't *turn* like you. Ah, here we are.'

Linus wasn't sure. Ever since he could fly (which, being a swift, was the first day of his life) he'd studied the peregrines, and copied

them. Could he really unlearn all of that? Did he even want to?

They had arrived at an old oak tree. In the distance, through a small wood, they could see the old lighthouse of Dungeness that stood next to the wave-kissed shingly beach.

'Right, see the old lighthouse? That's what we're aiming for, Linus. I'm going to fly to the top of it and when I flap my wings, I want you to take off as fast as you can, through the trees. Then on my command, bank left sharpish, turn around the lighthouse and come into land.'

'Seems simple enough!' the swift replied. 'Piece of cake.'

If this was all there was to it, he'd be the best in the RBF in no time, he thought to himself.

Atticus flew off, dodging the trees. He picked up pace over the open ground and, executing a perfect turn, circled the tower and perched himself on top of the lighthouse. The swift couldn't help but be impressed.

Then, nodding to Linus, Atticus brought his wings down like he was starting a race.

The swift took off as fast as he could, darted through the trees like he was on a slalom racecourse and sped towards the structure. He made it to the lighthouse in no time.

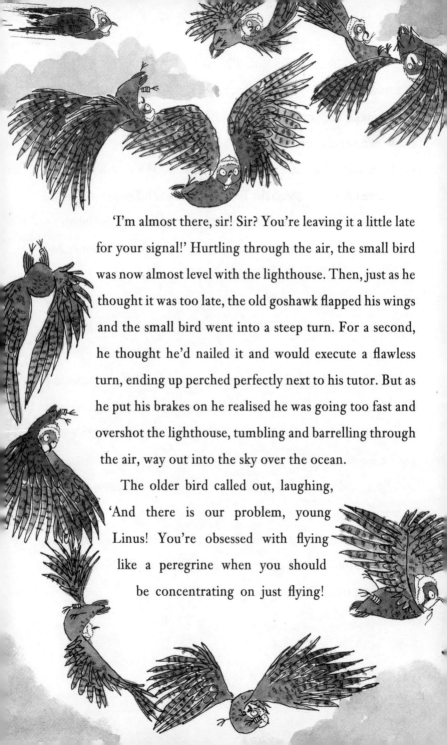

'I'm almost there, sir! Sir? You're leaving it a little late for your signal!' Hurtling through the air, the small bird was now almost level with the lighthouse. Then, just as he thought it was too late, the old goshawk flapped his wings and the small bird went into a steep turn. For a second, he thought he'd nailed it and would execute a flawless turn, ending up perched perfectly next to his tutor. But as he put his brakes on he realised he was going too fast and overshot the lighthouse, tumbling and barrelling through the air, way out into the sky over the ocean.

The older bird called out, laughing, 'And there is our problem, young Linus! You're obsessed with flying like a peregrine when you should be concentrating on just flying!

You swifts can turn, bank and screech . . . Oh, that awful sound you all make! Embrace who you are and stop trying to be someone else. No one ever said being in the RBF would be easy. Now, let's go again, and again, and again!'

Internally, Linus groaned. This wasn't what he'd signed up for; he WAS already a great flyer. All he needed was to fly with the peregrines and he'd show them. Still, Atticus was going out of his way to help, plus he was his superior, so he really didn't have a choice!

For the next few weeks, the old goshawk and the young swift woke up before first light and made their way to the old oak tree to train before their daily duties. Linus flew through the woods as fast as he could, ending at the lighthouse. At first he continued to overshoot the landing spot, out of breath, snagging twigs and branches along the way, building up too much speed and ending up spinning hopelessly out over the Channel.

Then, slowly at first, he gradually began to turn and bank like a swift, his turns became tighter and he recovered more quickly, until at last he could turn on a sixpence and come to perch right next to his teacher.

'Not bad at all, Master Linus. See, I told you, never mind those peregrines. You're a swift, and a blooming good one too. I don't think there's another bird in the RBF who can turn like you now.'

Linus had to admit, the training had done him the world of good. He missed Ava terribly, but he was holding tightly to the belief that she was safe and making her way to Tangled Wood. While he waited for her, flying with Atticus was the very best distraction; he felt fitter and more confident than he had done since he'd arrived. If he kept this up, they would surely let him fly on the front line, and maybe he would even get the respect of the falcons.

'Wanna bet on that?'

Master and student turned to see the peregrines of A-Squadron circling above. Marmaduke and Marcus flew down to confront them.

'From what I hear from my pals in the Canadian Geese Squadron, our friend Linus was a little too eager to take out a whole squadron . . . of his own birds!' Marmaduke said mockingly.

'You mind your own business, Marmaduke,' said Atticus. 'I seem to remember you scaring those starlings off the pier when you first signed up.'

'The sun was in my eyes! Anyway, any bird worth their salt knows that peregrines are the fastest there are.'

'Care to prove that?' asked Atticus.

'I'll take that bet,' answered Marcus.

'Er, boss, have you lost your mind?' Linus whispered to his mentor. 'I'm not sure I'm ready for this. Marmaduke is one thing, but Marcus! He's the fastest bird in the whole force, maybe in the country. I don't have a chance of beating him.'

'Have some faith. But yes, you make a good point, you've probably got no chance. Still, only one way to find out. Give it your best shot, eh?'

Linus gave Atticus a withering look. Atticus winked at him in return.

'Ahem, it's a straight race: slalom through the trees, a sprint to the lighthouse, one lap around then come to perch on the lantern room,' announced Atticus.

'The honour of the squadron is at stake, Linus, and you don't stand a chance!' Marcus said under his breath.

Linus didn't answer. All he could do was keep focused and remember what he'd been training for.

Trevor, a passing local woodpecker, volunteered to be the race starter. 'I was just pecking away looking for some insects

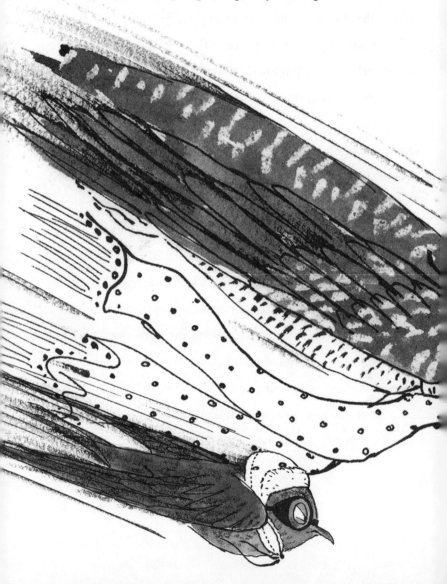

anyway, so happy to oblige. Always been a big fan of A-Squadron. Don't suppose I can get an autograph after?'

Atticus rolled his eyes and ushered the bird into position.

On the count of three loud pecks of the old oak – three . . . two . . . one . . . the birds were off.

Linus made an incredible start, nipping through the trees, instinctively arching and banking his body in the dense woodland, almost the way the majestic Spitfires played with the clouds.

Marcus, on the other hand, was struggling, knocking into twigs and branches, cursing as he went.

Breaking into the clearing, it was now a straight race to the lighthouse. Linus looked behind him but the falcon was nowhere to be seen. *I can't believe it; I'm going to win!* Linus thought as the lighthouse drew closer. But the falcon wasn't giving up that easily. Finally escaping the woods, Marcus quickly gained some height and then did what falcons do better than any other bird. Pinning his wings back, he went into a steep dive, gaining super-fast speed and making up lost ground on the swift.

Linus heard the whoosh before he saw

anything. Looking up, he saw what looked like a torpedo racing towards him. 'I told you, swift! The honour of the squadron is at stake. I can't lose to you!' Marcus screeched.

Linus tried with all his might, but there was no way he could match the extreme speed of a peregrine in a dive. He was still fifty metres ahead though. If he could just hold out for a few more seconds . . .

The top of the lantern room was coming up fast. Linus could see Atticus and now the rest of his squadron who had turned up (even a bleary-eyed Tyrone the owl) cheering him on. He could make it, he just knew he could.

Slowing down to bank around the tower he looked behind him to see the peregrine close and gaining ground, but he knew that Marcus had left it too late. All Linus had to do was round the tower and come to settle on top of the lighthouse and the race was won. He was just about to make the final turn, when *BOOM* – he felt an impact on his back that knocked the air out of his lungs. Spinning through the air, he wasn't even sure which way was up.

He shook his head and looked around to see that he was still airborne, half a mile out to sea. The rest of the birds were still perched around the lighthouse. He'd obviously collided with

Marcus and the impact had driven them both out into the skies above the Channel. But where was he now?

Looking around, he could make out the falcon a few hundred feet out to sea, but, oddly, he was still diving. Linus took off after him. 'Marcus! MARCUS!' he screeched. But the falcon was unresponsive.

That's not good, not good at all, Linus thought. In the collision, the peregrine must have knocked himself out and was now hurtling towards the sea. If the swift didn't act now . . . Marcus was done for.

7

Linus sped through the air, descending rapidly to catch up with the falcon, who was dropping like a stone. The sea below them was coming up fast.

'Marcus! Wake up, Marcus!' Linus screamed through the noise of the wind.

It was no good. Linus knew he had to act quickly. Positioning himself under the larger bird, so the falcon was lying on his back, he strained with all his might and tried to pull them both out of the steep dive, but Marcus was so heavy. The sea was coming closer and closer, and it felt like there was no way he could do it. With one final effort he felt their speed lessen, and gradually he was able to pull up so they were gliding just a few feet above the ocean. The peregrine began to come to.

'Urgh . . . Where am I?' he said groggily. 'I was going so fast . . . I collided into . . . Linus!' He looked around and realised he was alone with his rival, lying on the smaller bird's back.

Marcus might have been proud, but he was no fool and quickly worked out that the swift had saved him.

'Sir, is there any chance you could get off now you're awake?' Linus asked. 'You are VERY heavy!'

'Oh, sorry. I see we both took quite the tumble, and . . . and you saved my life. Trust me, I know I'd have ended up in the drink if not for you.' The peregrine looked more than a little embarrassed as he hopped off Linus's back. It seemed like he was about to apologise, but Linus interrupted him.

'Marcus, sir, over there!' The swift pointed his wings to a group of three or four aircraft about a mile or so into the Channel, heading towards France.

'By josh, you've got good eyes!' Marcus said. 'Looks like a German bomber with a fighter escort and one of our Spitfires in pursuit. Well, shall we?'

'Shouldn't we fly back and get the rest of the squadron?' Linus asked.

The falcon shook his head. 'By the time we get back the enemy

will be home safe and sound. This is down to you and me. Are you ready?'

This was it – finally his chance to fly with the elite in battle, to prove himself in combat, what he'd always dreamed of.

'Roger that, leader!' Linus smiled, excitement coursing through his veins.

'Then follow me.'

The birds gained altitude quickly and then, catching up with the dogfight, they surveyed the situation. The RAF Spitfire chasing the bomber had its hands full with the two German fighters, who were buzzing and harassing the Allied plane. The Spitfire got one of the Messerschmitts in his sights and the familiar *rat-tat-tat* of the Browning machine gun sounded as a trail of grey smoke started to appear from one of the German fighters.

'One down, two to go,' cried Marcus. 'Let's make for that bomber.'

The birds sped through the air and positioned themselves so they were flying directly over the German plane.

'What do we do?' cried Linus above the noise. 'We have nothing to drop on it – no sticks or stones!'

'Oh no, we have something much better and far more fun.

Watch and learn, Linus!' Marcus winked mischievously.

Linus watched as the speedy falcon flew directly over the cockpit of the huge German plane and, with perfect accuracy, pooped all over the pilot's window, completely obscuring his view. Then he banked away in fits of laughter to join Linus and survey his handiwork.

'Like I always say: in poo we trust! Now your turn!'

The agile swift followed the Squadron Leader's example and, with near-perfect aim, dropped his . . . *droppings* on to the cockpit of the bomber.

'*Voila!* Excellent work! Gets me every time! The pilots always look so confused – one minute, a crystal-blue sky all around them; the next, a windscreen full of bird poo,' chuckled Marcus.

Sure enough, before the pilot and crew could work out what had happened to them, the Spitfire had zeroed in on the hapless bomber and opened fire, hitting its target. One of the engines had started to smoke and the plane made a rapid descent, looking for a safe place to crash-land.

Ginger Thomas rubbed his eyes in disbelief. One minute he was involved in a dogfight with two Messerschmitt 109s, one of which he'd despatched. The next minute he'd looked up to see the bomber he was originally after was flying erratically, now directly in his sights. He opened up his deadly 303 machine guns and saw smoke coming from the stricken bomber, which peeled away looking for a safe place to crash-land.

Satisfied he'd done enough, Ginger glanced to his right and saw the cockpit covered in bird poo and two small birds banking and rolling as if in celebration.

I AM going crazy . . . bird crazy, he thought. With this; that downed Messerschmitt earlier in the summer; and then last month, as he was walking through town to his billet from the pub, he'd sworn he'd seen a bird, a large bird, a buzzard or some such, flapping around the windows and the blackout curtains by the town hall. The same town hall that was bombed that very night!

That's it, he thought. *I'm going mad. Time to put in for some leave.*

He checked the skies around him. The other Messerschmitt was nowhere to be seen, and he was getting low on fuel and ammo. He gratefully headed for home.

Distracted by the action, the two birds realised they were now over a coastline.

'Goodness gracious, I lost track of where we are. I think we're

over France! We'd better head for home!' Marcus yelled.

The birds started to bank and head back for the English coast, when the crackle of machine-gun fire zipped through the air. The pair looked around, thinking they were about to be caught up in a dogfight between the remaining German plane and the Spitfire, but far off they could see the RAF fighter making for home.

'He must be low on fuel,' said Marcus.

'Yes,' gulped Linus. 'But if the German isn't shooting at him . . .'

'He must be shooting at US!' Marcus finished Linus's sentence for him.

Unbelievably, the birds were right. With the Spitfire heading for home, and having seen the pesky birds unload their bombs of poo on the bomber, the German fighter pilot had had enough and was now hunting down the birds.

'Quick, dive! Make for that bridge!' Marcus pointed to a small railway bridge a few hundred feet below them. The pair of birds went into a steep dive with the German plane in hot pursuit. 'We should be safe when we get under there,' Marcus shouted as a hail of machine-gun fire whistled past them.

'I think I might have been a bit hasty in wanting to join your

squadron!' said Linus. 'The carrier pigeons might have been a better idea!'

'You're not alone there! But we're not done for yet!'

The birds made it to the safety of the underside of the bridge just as the brickwork was peppered with machine-gun fire. They looked up to see the German plane heading right for the bridge, but he was so fixated on chasing the birds, he had left it too late to pull up. The plane clipped the top of the bridge. The birds watched as smoke came from the engine as it disappeared over a canopy of trees, the pilot lucky to have survived. He wasn't the only one.

'Jeez! That was lucky!' panted Linus.

'Yes, not exactly how I thought today would go!' said Marcus.

'Now, we need to find shelter. I have no idea who we can trust, and a passing swift and a falcon will stick out like a sore thumb, so we'd best find a place to hide and rest, before we work out when to fly home. I think I spotted a barn about half a mile from here. Shall we try that?'

With the German plane gone, the skies were clear and Linus had a brief moment to take a look around him as they flew.

The criss-cross fields were surrounded by tall hedgerows, and as he looked out to sea he noticed the powerful and foreboding

battery guns that pointed towards home, reminding him that they would have to proceed with caution.

Sure enough, just as Marcus had spotted, a well-maintained hay-lined barn was a welcome sight for the birds. It stood alongside a stone farmhouse where a smoking chimney and the smell of a stew boiling away somewhere in the kitchen made Linus think of the farm he grew up in in England; they were the same people, facing the same struggle. And now here he was on the front line helping them. Ava would be proud of him, of that he was sure. He choked back a tear and followed the larger bird down to take a look.

Marcus had found a small abandoned nest in the eaves. After such an eventful day, both the birds were exhausted, and although unlikely bed mates they got settled side by side.

'Are you OK?' asked the falcon. 'That was quite the adventure.'

'You know, sir, all I've ever wanted, since I was a chick, was to fly with an elite squadron like yours. To "Fly with the Peregrines". It's all I ever talked about. But I never thought I'd be actually shot at. I'm not sure I was ready for that!' Linus chuckled.

'Well, to start with, for now at least you can drop the "sir". Call me Marcus. And let me assure you, pooing on enemy planes and then being fired upon isn't exactly a cakewalk. You acquitted

yourself brilliantly today and,' he stared at the ground, 'I need to thank you for saving my life. That was both a brilliant piece of flying and a remarkable display of bravery.'

Linus blushed. He couldn't believe that at the beginning of the day the falcons had viewed him as a joke, and now one of the best flyers in the land was singing his praises.

The dashing young peregrine Squadron Leader seemed to sense his mood, and was eager to make amends.

'Also, I'd like to apologise to you, Linus. My squadron and I have treated you badly. You are an incredible flyer, and you've travelled halfway around the world to join the fight. That counts for a lot. As for Marmaduke, I'm sorry about him too. I've known him ever since we were chicks and he's always been very protective of me. I'll have a word with him when we get back to base. You'll see a change in the whole squadron, I promise.'

It took all of Linus's composure for his beak not to fall on the floor in disbelief, but he could see that the peregrine was genuine, and wanted to talk more.

'Er, thanks. Do you mind me asking, was it always what you wanted to do as well . . . to fly, to fight?' he ventured.

'To be honest, I don't know. I never really had a choice. My

father flew in the last war. He won the Dickin Medal, the highest honour an animal can be given by a human. He works in London now, high up in the Animal Air Ministry. My grandfather flew in the war before that, and even my great-grandparents helped smuggle seed to feed carrier pigeons for the French in the Franco-Prussian War. Service is all my family have ever known. Quite what they'll think if we fall into enemy hands doesn't bear thinking about. What about you?'

'I'm from a family of racers. Swifts are always on the move, so we don't own much but we've always been fast! I've only ever wanted to fly with the best. That's you, by the way,' he smiled. Marcus blushed. 'So my sister and I signed up to protect our homelands. And QUITE what she'd make of ME falling into enemy hands doesn't bear thinking about either. She was supposed to be here with me, but she's missing in action.'

Marcus smiled sympathetically. 'I'm sorry to hear that, Linus, but don't lose hope. If she's anything like her brother, I like her odds of survival. I guess we're not so different after all, different backgrounds, but born to fly. Now, my new-found friend, we need a plan to get out of here.'

Linus nodded intently.

'It's dark now. I think that at first light we make a dash for it, and stay low. There's no point splitting up – that's even more dangerous, but peregrines and swifts aren't exactly bedfellows, so we will stick out. Plus, we'll have to hope our bats can pick us up on their radar and send out an escort party if we get into trouble. For now, let's get some rest and—'

Marcus was interrupted by a creak at the barn door.

They were not alone.

8

Poking their heads above the nest they saw a group of shapes moving by candlelight. The light was dim, but the birds could see the straw-covered barn floor, and four animals and one bird lurking in the shadows. It was clear to Linus that they didn't want to be spotted, so were almost certainly up to no good. He sensed danger as he heard his tiny heart thump in his chest. He didn't mind admitting (at least to himself) that he was more than a little scared. Marcus interrupted his thoughts.

'Blast!' he whispered. 'We're stuck like rats in a trap.'

The two birds stayed stock-still, so their presence would go undetected.

They heard a French accent from the barn floor.

'*Mon ami*, put Monsieur Speckles over there in the corner and

give him some seed while I work out our plan, but DON'T TAKE YOUR EYES OFF HIM! If he gets loose again, I'll have your stripes!'

'Great Scott!' whispered Marcus. 'That's Lord Speckles, one of the greatest carrier pigeons of all time. He must have been captured by these brigands. I'll bet they're working for the Germans. We have to do something.'

'Sure, but what?' hissed Linus. 'There's only two of us, and in case you hadn't noticed, my skill of "flying really fast" doesn't count for a lot in a barn.'

'The barn! That's the answer!' The peregrine flapped his wings excitedly as the idea came to him. 'Linus, do you see all the farm tools that are hung on the barn wall? Directly above those shadowy characters? On my command, fly as fast and as silently as you can and cut the tools free with your beak and claws. They'll land on them and I'll do the rest with my talons. OK?'

The swift nodded, excited and terrified in equal measure.

'Three – two – one – go!'

Linus took off as fast as he could. Quick as a flash and without a sound, he cut loose a collection of brooms, rakes and a wheelbarrow. From the shadows he could hear the *donks* of the tools hitting the unfortunate animals below and the enraged *ouch*es and *owww*s coming from the darkness.

He descended into the candlelit gloom to see a ferret, a badger and a mole all trapped beneath the farmyard tools. Marcus had a fox pinned beneath his talons.

'Surrender, you traitor!' the falcon demanded.

'Never,' the fox replied loudly. 'I fight for the glory of animal-kind and for France. *Vive la France!* It is you who are the traitor. Do with us what you will and go and serve your new masters.'

'Hang on,' said the peregrine, confused. He turned to the carrier pigeon, who had his beak in a plate of seed. 'Lord Speckles, haven't this lot captured you? Lord Speckles!'

'Oh, hello, Marcus.' The pigeon looked up from his dinner absent-mindedly. 'I say, smashing to see you. What are you doing here? I see you've met my French friends. They're just helping me out of a spot of bother.'

'Erm, he doesn't seem to be very worried *or* very captive,' said Linus.

'Yes, he does have a reputation for being a bit vague, but when he's flying with a message strapped to him, he's the best in the business – a national hero!'

The falcon looked down at the trapped fox beneath him, and immediately hopped off him, helping him back to his feet. 'Terribly sorry, old boy. I heard you come into the barn and feared the worst, what with you putting him in a corner under guard and all that.'

'Well, I can see why you'd think that, I suppose,' the fox answered, dusting himself down. 'But we had no choice but to keep him under guard – he keeps wandering off. Oh la la, he is, how would you say . . . a little crazy?'

'Yes, there's no argument there; the bird is as mad as a March hare. But tell us, what is going on here?'

'We are the Resistance, my friend! A group of animals working together to help thwart the Occupation. My name is Emmanuel, and this is Jean, Dimitri and Marie.' He introduced the ferret, the mole and the badger one by one, who nodded their greetings as they rubbed their sore heads.

The fox continued. 'We've been trying to get a message to your Air Ministry for days, and finally this pigeon arrived last night. He took flight with the message, but the Germans shot him – they are instructed to shoot at all carrier pigeons on sight – and his wing is injured. It's not too bad, but without support he cannot make it back. But now you, the British flyers, are here he can try to get the message back to your RBF and on to the humans.'

'What message? What's all the fuss about?' asked Linus.

'Encrypted messages,' Marcus answered. 'Pigeons are the only way to get official messages back to London. If it's not delivered by the wing of a pigeon, the Ministry will discount and ignore it.'

'And the fuss, my young swift,' said the fox, 'is about the largest air raid the Germans have ever launched, and it is due to take place tomorrow. If we can't get that encrypted secret message back to your Air Ministry and on to the humans . . . the battle in the air will almost certainly be lost! There is no time to lose! Come, let us show you what we have discovered.'

Under the still, moonlit sky, Emmanuel and his band of Resistance fighters quietly led the way through the fields to the edge of a massive airfield enclosed by a wire fence.

The birds could hear the drones of the aircraft overhead.

'Do you hear, my friends? Do you hear those mechanical beasts?' The fox shook his head in sorrow. 'Our best diggers, Dimitri and Marie, dug under the fence and heard of the German's plans.' The mole and the badger nodded ruefully.

'It's true. See for yourself,' the badger sighed.

It was a tight squeeze, but the two birds hopped through the tunnel dug by Dimitri and Marie and popped out the other side to see for themselves.

Sure enough, hundreds of planes – bombers and fighters – were being fuelled up. Most were under camouflage so the human planes couldn't spot them from the air.

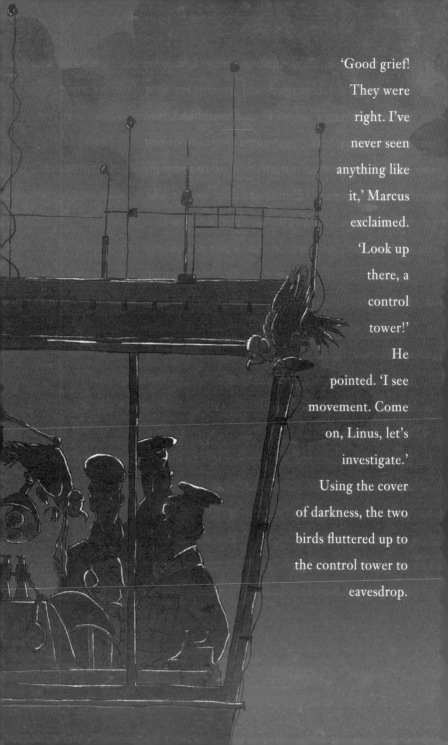

'Good grief! They were right. I've never seen anything like it,' Marcus exclaimed. 'Look up there, a control tower!' He pointed. 'I see movement. Come on, Linus, let's investigate.' Using the cover of darkness, the two birds fluttered up to the control tower to eavesdrop.

Hearts thudding, they peeked through a window. A meeting was taking place between several men dressed in the distinctive blue-grey uniform of the Luftwaffe. Was this where the raid was being planned?

Marcus brought his wing up to his beak to indicate that Linus should stay silent. The young swift nodded and they listened.

'But we have no proof the RAF are on their knees; this raid could be a disaster,' one of the enemy was arguing.

'The Commander-in-Chief is insisting it goes ahead as planned tomorrow. We have reliable intelligence from our spies on where to bomb all along the south coast, thanks to this bird who delivered their messages.' He gestured to the corner of the room where a bird was in the darkness.

Marcus and Linus stared at each other. 'The traitor is in there!' Marcus whispered furiously. 'We have to find out who it is!'

'Yes, but surely it's more important to get home and raise the alarm? If we get caught, Lord Speckles never gets home,' Linus argued.

The falcon nodded. 'Blast, you're right, the traitor will have to wait. My father said the Allies have been talking about this raid, but they don't think it will be for ages! If they destroy the RAF in the skies, there won't be enough planes to defend Britain from the air and the enemy will be able to invade on land. We have to act now.'

The birds sped back to find their Resistance friends.

'Let's get out of here and get Speckles home!' Linus urged. But before they could move they saw the bright glare of torchlight illuminating them.

They'd been spotted.

A young soldier was aiming his rifle right at them. 'Ah, breakfast!' he smiled to himself.

As the man raised the gun, Linus knew he'd never take off in time – he was a goner. He shut his eyes and waited.

'Arrrggghhh!' the young German cried out. Linus opened his eyes to see Dimitri and Marie with their teeth around his ankles.

'Fly, my friends!' the mole shouted with glee.

The birds took off and flew back over the fence as the small mammals chased off the German, who was clutching his throbbing ankle as he ran.

'Thanks!' Linus said to Emmanuel as they scampered and flew back to the barn. 'You were right. If we don't get this information back to London, the war could be lost in days! It will be light soon. We need to get a move on, before it's too late.'

9

'Oh, Lord Speckles . . . Lord Speckles!' Linus chirped at the fast-asleep bird. 'Time to get up! We have a message to deliver and a world to save . . . Lord Speckles . . . LORD SPECKLES!'

The confused pigeon woke with a start and looked around the barn.

'Oh, I'm frightfully sorry, dear boy! Absolutely exhausted! Now, what was it you wanted?'

Linus looked at Marcus in exasperation.

'My Lord, our friends here have told us you have a message, a secret encrypted message, that might be . . . could be . . . quite important to the war effort.'

'Ah yes,' said the sleepy pigeon, straining to remember. 'I do recall something like that . . . but I'm afraid the old wing is a bit

busted up. Can't fly for toffee. Only way to get home would be to be carried, and who'd be crazy enough to do that?'

Linus and Marcus looked at each other.

'Well, don't look at me!' said Linus. 'You were heavy enough, and he's as big as a hen house!'

'Arrgghhh,' groaned the falcon. 'Come on then, climb aboard!'

Emmanuel and his band had led the birds to a clearing a few hundred metres inland, near to a sea cliff.

'Right, My Lord, no matter what happens, hold on tight. If you fall off I don't think I'll have the strength to get you back up, and you'll end up in the drink. Linus, you lead the way, and keep your eyes peeled for the enemy.'

The fox shook their wings warmly. 'Good luck, my friends, and thank you. Lord Speckles, the fate of the free world – animal *and* human – is in your hands. *Bonne chance!*'

The three birds waved their comrades goodbye and took flight, with Linus scouting ahead, alert for the enemy.

Soaring ahead, the little swift had, at last, time on his own to reflect on the last crazy twenty-four hours. He'd gone from being the joke of the squadron to saving the life of, and now flying with, the most famous and renowned bird in the RBF. What's more,

he was respected and admired by him, and they were friends! And now here he was at the front of the formation. Yes, he was nervous, but he wasn't scared any more. He knew what needed to be done, and he wasn't going to let anyone down. If only Ava was there to share it all, he thought with a sharp pang of sadness. But he pushed it away. He had to focus on the mission ahead – it's what she'd want him to do.

The plan was to fly east along the coastline, then when the Channel was at its narrowest, they'd make a break for it to try to get back to base, raise the alarm, then continue on to London to help Lord Speckles deliver the message to the Air Ministry.

While they skirted the coast of northern France, they could stay under the cover of the cliffs and trees. The Resistance fighters had told them of squadrons of wasps patrolling the cliffs around the coastline, but apart from a couple of distant swarms, Linus didn't come across any. Before long, the young swift saw a large port town up ahead.

'That's Calais!' he shouted back to the others. It was the first town he'd seen in France when making his long migration to his winter home in Africa.

'Good work, Linus,' Marcus yelled. 'Now's the time to turn north.

Remember, we'll
need to stay low. If we're
spotted we'll be sitting ducks. Well, sitting
birds, really . . . OK, ready? Let's make a break for it!'

The birds struck out across the open water of the Channel.
Skimming just above the waves they could feel the spray of the
ocean wet their beaks, and, glancing down, Linus could see a pod
of blue and white bottlenose dolphins below them, keeping pace.

'We can climb in a minute,' Marcus yelled over the roar of the
wind. 'Catch the thermals and we'll be back to base in no time.'

The crack of a machine gun shattered their thoughts of home.
Linus looked around in a panic, confused about where the sound

had come from. They were clear of the coast, too far out to be in range of any coastal defences. He turned his head behind him to see the deadly shape of an E-boat in pursuit. A keen-eyed sailor had obviously spotted Lord Speckles and alerted the captain to the presence of a carrier pigeon. The boat was now charging towards them and the machine guns were slowly zeroing in on their target.

'They've spotted Speckles,' Marcus yelled. 'The Germans know the pigeons carry vital messages, so they will try to shoot him – and us – down!'

'This is quite intolerable!' complained Lord Speckles from his perch on Marcus's back. 'I mean, can't we all just sit down and talk it through?'

'He really isn't all there, is he?' shouted Linus.

'I'm afraid not, but we won't be either if we don't come up with something!' said Marcus. 'We can't just climb! We'll be shot down too easily.'

Machine-gun fire whistled past them, getting ever closer.

The small swift looked behind him and saw the huge German boat bearing down on them, cutting easily through the waves that were getting bigger the further they got into the Channel.

Waves . . . that's it! thought Linus.

'I've got an idea!' he shouted. 'It might not work . . . I mean, we could drown, or at best get soaking wet!'

Lord Speckles grimaced. 'Oh, I say, old boy, I don't know about that. I'm not the biggest fan of—'

'I'm all ears!' interrupted Marcus. 'Soaking wet sounds just fine compared to that gunfire! I can't fly at this speed much longer with Speckles on my back.'

'OK, this is going to sound crazy! I think we should fly into the crest of the biggest wave we can find. If we make it out the other side – big "if"! – we climb straight away. The spray from the wave should give us enough cover to make our ascent . . . maybe. What do you reckon?'

Both the other birds looked at Linus as if he had lost his mind, but they nodded their heads, as they had little choice.

'OK, there's a huge wave up ahead! Follow me!' Linus screeched as more machine-gun fire just missed them. 'Ready . . . Take a deep breath and fly as hard as you can . . . Go!'

All three birds ploughed into the crest of the wave. The power of the icy water knocked the air out of the swift's lungs. For a second that felt like an eternity it seemed like the force of the wave would engulf them and they would be dragged crashing down with no hope, but with one last push Linus found himself the other side of the mountain of water and climbing as fast as his wings could carry him. He looked to his side to see the soaking-wet, but still airborne, shapes of his two comrades next to him.

Looking behind them, they could see the huge wave crashing into the E-boat. The spray engulfed the wheelhouse, then, as they emerged from the wave, they saw the crew frantically scouring the horizon in search of their quarry. But Linus, Marcus and Lord Speckles were already harmlessly out of range.

'Well, that was unconventional,' said Marcus, 'but also total GENIUS! Well done, Linus! Now, let's get back to base, get Lord Speckles' wing patched up and then onwards to London!'

10

Not even the cockerel had stirred by the time the birds reached the safety of their base. They landed in the middle of the farmyard, guided by the smouldering fire, and, with a groan, Marcus helped Lord Speckles down, where he immediately set about devouring scattered grain from the last night's dinner.

Marcus turned to Linus. 'We've no time to lose. I'll go and wake Wing Commander Butler. You send for a team of field-mice medics – and wake up Atticus!' he yelled as he flew towards HQ.

Linus started to fly over to the medical building to rouse the mice, but a sound to his left distracted him. He turned to see Marmaduke emerge from his barn, looking at the swift suspiciously.

'Oh, I see you're back! We feared the worst. Where's Marcus?'

'He's gone to wake Wing Commander Butler. Lord Speckles

here needs some medical attention, then we must take flight to London urgently. Can you help?'

'Of course. You wake Atticus, then join me at the sick bay. Then we'll work out what do to about this German raid.'

Linus turned to go but something the falcon had said stopped him in his tracks.

'But I didn't say anything about a German raid . . .' he muttered, half to himself. 'I just said we need to get to London.' He turned and met the gaze of the falcon, and in that moment Linus knew without doubt who had been the traitor leaking the secrets to the Germans. *Marmaduke*.

Quick as lightning the falcon grabbed poor Lord Speckles and

lifted a razor-sharp talon to his throat. 'Another flap of your wings, Linus, and the pigeon gets it!'

'I say, steady on, old thing! If you wanted to share my breakfast, all you had to do was ask!' the potty old pigeon complained.

'Marmaduke!' Marcus shouted from the door of HQ. 'What are you doing?'

Linus saw his friend's expression change as the horror of what was happening dawned on him.

'It was you all along? We've been fighting together all these last months . . . We were eggs together! And you're a . . . a *traitor*?'

'Oh, don't be so surprised!' scorned Marmaduke. 'You're so full of yourself, it's a wonder you even know I exist! Do you have any idea what it's like to live in your shadow? Marcus *this* and Marcus *that*! Ever since we were chicks I've been your second, your *wingman*. I'm a good flyer . . . a GREAT flyer! But I never get the respect I deserve.'

'So it was you who led the Germans to the town hall the night I arrived, and it was you in the control tower at the airfield,' deduced Linus.

'Of course it was me. I don't care about the humans, British *or* German, or who wins this stupid war. This is about ME! So

when I got approached by a double agent – a gannet, as it happens, absolutely charming chap – I jumped at the chance.

'I've been guiding enemy planes in for weeks. With the Germans in charge and you out of the way, I'll finally get the respect and recognition I deserve. My own squadron! Maybe even a wing!

'It was all going according to plan until this pipsqueak rumbled me,' he said bitterly, gesturing to Linus. 'Still, no matter! After today there won't be much left of the RBF *or* the RAF. Now, I'm flying back to France with Speckles and none of you are going to stop me, or – well, these talons are *awfully sharp* . . .'

Lord Speckles looked a bit green. 'I don't mean to moan and I'm *awfully* grateful for all your help, but I . . . I don't think I can face another trip across the Channel . . .'

'Quiet, you blithering idiot!' Marmaduke snapped. He edged further out of the farmyard. HQ was slowly coming to life, woken by the commotion, and bleary birds and mammals started poking their heads out of barn doors.

Starting to panic, Marmaduke edged backwards. 'Stay back! All of you! There isn't a bird here fast enough to stop me. Stay back, or the pigeon gets it!'

But Linus knew there *was* one bird who could stop Marmaduke.

He looked over at Marcus, to see his look of dejection had been replaced by a steely resolve.

Returning his stare, the peregrine falcon gave the slightest of nods. It was all Linus needed to see.

Turning to the increasingly panicked Marmaduke, he calculated the ground he needed to cover, and then with one huge effort, Linus took flight.

He launched through the air, and his speed took the falcon by surprise. Linus covered the distance between them in no time, knocking the falcon's talons away and allowing the hapless Lord Speckles to scramble to safety on a nearby post.

Linus, though, was anything but safe. The furious falcon turned his anger on the little swift, pinning him to the floor. With his talons raised, he leered down at the tiny bird.

'You idiot! You've changed nothing! The attack will still go ahead, you'll still be wiped off the earth and out of the skies . . .' He drew his talons back. 'I should have done this the first night we met!'

Linus shut his eyes, terror gripping his heart.

But the deadly blow never came. Just at that moment, Marmaduke was bundled on to his back and held down by Marcus,

Atticus and some very spirited mice.

Wing Commander Butler had arrived in time to witness the fracas. Now he stood over Linus, offering him his wing. 'I think we might have misjudged you, Master Linus. That was quite the bravest thing I've seen in some time. Take the traitor away!'
A dangerous-looking platoon of shifty-eyed stoats dragged the still-raging falcon off to a birdcage in the stables.

'Thank you, sir,' said Linus, dusting himself down 'But we have no time to waste! We need to get Lord Speckles and his encrypted message to the Air Ministry – and FAST! I'm worried we might already be too late.
If our fears are correct, there's a whole day of air attacks coming, the likes of which we've never seen before. The humans must be warned!'

'Then go!' the Wing Commander ordered. 'We'll hold the fort here. Get back as soon as you can!'

Minutes later, Marcus, Linus and a bandaged-up Lord Speckles took off, bound for the Air Ministry in London.

Linus could feel the adrenalin pumping through his wings. The whole country was relying on them to deliver Lord Speckles' message. They just didn't know it yet. And if they were too late, the war could be lost before it had even truly begun.

II

Picking up the warm air that rushed over the south of England, the three birds took no time at all in getting to the capital. Before long they saw smoke rising from the chimneys, and the smouldering docks of east London, where an enemy bombing raid had evidently taken place the night before.

By now, the sun had just about broken and although early in the day, Marcus had said he knew the Animal Air Ministry would be abuzz with activity.

The Ministry was nestled in the roof of one of the many human government buildings on Whitehall – a long, tree-lined street of brilliant-white-walled buildings. Bookended by Nelson's Column at one end and the Houses of Parliament at the other, it was an intimidating sight. Linus's eyes popped as they

looked for a place to land.

'I didn't know humans could build anything this big!' Linus couldn't get over the enormous size of everything in this city. 'And are you sure the Air Marshal will listen? There's only three of us, and I'm not sure Lord Speckles is the bird I'd want to rely on, given the circumstances. No disrespect, My Lord!'

'Oh, none taken, dear boy. I say, do you think I might be excused? My club is just around the corner and I hear they're serving suet balls today.'

'Yeah . . . not yet? If that's OK?' said Marcus. We might need you and that encrypted message from the Resistance to, you know, help save the world?'

'Oh, jolly good!'

'You're right,' whispered Marcus to Linus. 'He's a few twigs short of a nest. We can't let him do any of the talking or they'll think we're mad. Leave that to me. Ah, here we are.'

Marcus had spotted a ledge just below the eaves of the building. It was a hive of activity, with all manner of birds flying to and fro – robins, blackbirds, magpies, starlings, all seemingly in a huge hurry. Two pigeons in police uniform stood guard next to the main window where the birds landed.

'Oi, you three!' said one of them. 'No landing here. This ledge is for authorised military aviators only.'

'What do you think this is?' said Marcus confidently, pointing to the stripes on his ring. 'I'm a Squadron Leader, on the front line! A-Squadron, Flight Group 11, South Coast. You have to let us through on a matter of the utmost urgency.'

'I'm very sorry, sir, but orders is orders. Where's your pass? No entry unless authorised and signed by order of Air Vice-Marshal Falco.'

'But I'm his SON, Marcus Falco!'

'Ah, well, anyone could say that, couldn't they, Stan?' the police pigeon said to his partner.

'You're not wrong there, Ernie. What's to say you lot aren't enemy spies masquerading as our RBF boys?'

'If we win this war it'll be a miracle,' an exasperated Marcus muttered under his breath to Linus. He tried one last time. 'Look, can someone *please* find Air Vice-Marshal Falco and tell him that his SON is here with Lord Speckles and a very important message.'

'Oh, my. Stone the crows. No Ern, not literally!' said Stan as his bird-brained partner Ernie went to throw a stone at a passing crow.

'Lord Speckles? Why didn't you say so? Oh, sir, this is indeed an

honour, that we two humble, God-fearing, everyday rock pigeons should meet a hero like yourself! Why, I used to have pictures of you on me wall, sir. You inspired me to sign up, truth be told. I'd do anything to join the carrier pigeon corps. Do you think you could put a good word in for me?'

Marcus saw an opportunity. 'Yes! Yes, he most certainly could! COULDN'T YOU, Lord Speckles?'

The famous pigeon looked at them all absent-mindedly. 'Oh, yes, of course, old thing, happy to oblige,' he said vaguely.

'See, you'll get the call-up papers at the end of the week. Now, any chance we can see the Air Vice-Marshal?' said Marcus.

'Of course, sir, certainly, sir, right this way.' The police pigeon bowed and led them through the window to a corridor lined with paintings of falcons, buzzards and eagles, all of whom had served in the Air Ministry at one time or another.

'Some of them do look an awful lot like you, Marcus,' Linus observed.

'Well, that stands to reason. I'm related to most of them!'

They came to a door at the end of the corridor. The police pigeon knocked on the door and had a quick word with an impatient and busy-looking squirrel carrying folders under its arm,

who eyed the tired, dishevelled-looking trio with scepticism. It disappeared for a minute and then came back. 'The Air Vice-Marshal says he will be with you in just a moment.' The pigeon bowed reverentially and returned to his post, muttering to himself as he went, 'THE Lord Speckles . . . if the boys in the coop could see me now . . .'

The birds perched for a couple of minutes, trying not to let the fatigue get the better of them and succumb to sleep, before the door opened and an enormous falcon emerged.

'Father!' said Marcus, hopping to his feet. 'We have some urgent news!'

'Marcus, my dear boy! Wonderful to see you!' His father beamed. 'Are you on leave? Have you been down to see your mother? She'll be livid if you've come to see me first. We can't catch any fowl, what with the war on, but I'm sure she can rustle up something special. Now, I can't spare much time, very busy, but the good news is, our intelligence is saying that big German raid won't happen for weeks. We sent a squadron of high-flying swans over and they've seen nothing, so we're not too worried. I say, how about some eggs? The mess will be open in just a tick. Now, before that, come and see the operations room. This is where you'd work, in the centre

of it all, if you'd finally agree to come and join me.'

The young falcon tried to protest, but his father hushed him and ushered the birds through a heavy door. A balcony ran around the top of the room, connected to the floor below by two staircases. The floor was dominated by a map of northern France and the south of England. A group of squirrels in uniform were busy plotting the map with miniature model birds.

'The operations room! And as you and your friends can see,

everything is under control. Now, how about I introduce you to some of the top birds and we have that breakfast.'

'No! Father! Listen! That's why we're here. There *is* an attack planned today. The Resistance helped us escape to bring you an encrypted message carried by Lord Speckles.'

The pigeon unclipped the note from his leg and handed it to the old falcon, who unfolded and read it. He contemplated it for a minute and then eyed his son's companions with an air of caution.

He put his wing around his son and ushered him a few feet away from the others.

'Listen, my boy, I'm not sure about all this. Our intelligence is pretty sound. Plus, the Resistance are a rum old lot at the best of times. Run by foxes, for goodness' sake! And as for that pigeon, he lost his marbles after the last war and he's never been the same since. I'm not sure how much stock we can put in his word.'

'You're wrong!' piped up Linus.

The enormous falcon turned to fix his gaze on the tiny bird. Marcus looked on in horror.

'And who might you be?'

'Er, Linus the swift . . . er, B-Squadron, Flight Group II . . .'

'Right, and does Linus the swift, B-Squadron, Flight Group II understand the concept of *rank*?'

Linus winced. He knew he shouldn't interrupt a superior officer – but this was too important! 'I'm sorry, sir, truly – permission to speak?'

'Hmm,' the falcon sighed. 'Very well. Go on.'

Linus took a deep breath and spoke very quickly. 'Well, er, sir, your son is telling the truth. You see, we did see German planes – scores of them – on the coast of France, and our lives were saved by these brilliant Resistance fighters: a fox, a badger, a ferret and a mole. And I know Lord Speckles is a little daft, but he is a legend, and we got shot at by a plane and a boat, and your son, oh my word, he was amazing, he brought down a German bomber all on his own, with his poo . . . his own poo! So what I'm trying to say is . . . you have to listen to us!'

The falcon peered over his glasses at the tiny swift and then looked at his son, who nodded earnestly.

'It's true, Father, every word. And Linus is the best I've flown with – he's the fastest, the bravest, and he saved my life . . .'

That stopped the Air Vice-Marshal in his tracks. 'Really?'

Linus nodded, a little embarrassed.

'I'd be dead without him,' explained Marcus. 'So you have to listen to us. The Germans WILL attack today.'

'Marcus, my boy, if we send this to the humans and you are wrong, they will never trust using a carrier pigeon again. The Animal Air Ministry will be finished and we'll be a laughing stock. Are you one hundred per cent sure?'

Both Linus and Marcus nodded.

'Yes, yes, at least fifty per cent sure, old chap!' Lord Speckles added vaguely.

The older falcon closed his eyes. 'Very well, but I'm putting my beak on the line. Wait here.'

He hopped down to the map floor below and went into a deep conversation with an enormous golden eagle and a bulldog wearing a top hat.

'Oh my . . .' The colour drained from Marcus's face.

'What?' asked Linus.

'That's Air Chief Marshal Talon and Sir Bertie Bulldog – the animal Prime Minister!'

The three animals conferred for what seemed like an eternity and then nodded to each other in agreement.

The Air Vice-Marshal cried out, 'Pigeon! I need a carrier pigeon immediately. Urgent message for number ten Downing Street. Action this day!'

Suddenly the room came alive with telephones ringing and orders chirped across the grand space.

'You've done it!' said Linus. 'They're passing the message to the humans!'

'*We've* done it,' answered Marcus, with an exhausted smile.

They looked down at the floor below just as the old bulldog glanced up at them. Holding their gaze for a second, he gave them the tiniest nod of gratitude and then left the room.

Air Vice-Marshal Falco flew up to join them. 'Well, my boy, the cat is among the pigeons now. Figure of speech!' he added, as Lord Speckles gulped loudly. 'Listen, I'm sorry I doubted you, Linus. You must all stay here today. You look exhausted.'

'Sorry, Father, but we've got a war to fight out there. Can you look after poor old Lord Speckles though? I think he's seen quite enough action for one day.'

'Gladly! Good luck, my boy, be safe, and the same to you, young Linus. This looks to be a day like no other.'

The two birds saluted and waved goodbye, and then they were off to face the biggest challenge of their young lives.

12

The young friends got back to Tangled Wood Airfield in no time. With everything that had happened in the last twenty-four hours, Linus didn't have time to be nervous or scared. This was everything he'd dreamed about as a little chick. Here he was about to enter into the hardest battle of his life. He was flying with the best, but now he was one of the best too. He was a swift, and proud of it. The only thing he regretted was that Ava wasn't flying alongside him. Right now, though, there wasn't any time for sadness; this long day would need all the focus he could muster.

He was looking forward to seeing Atticus and his squadron, but as they flew over the hill to the north of the airfield, the sight they were met with sent chills down their spines.

The green fields of the airstrip were replaced by bomb craters,

and the control tower had been obliterated. The birds saw a squadron of Hurricanes dodging the enormous potholes as they taxied to take off.

'This is bad,' chirped Marcus quietly. 'I hope we haven't been clobbered as well.'

As the birds flew over the treetops and caught sight of the farmhouse, it was plain to see it hadn't been spared the onslaught. The windows had been blown out, and one of the walls had a huge hole in it. The pigeons' barn had all but been destroyed and the bats' stable had collapsed.

'Thank goodness you're back!' Wing Commander Butler squawked at the pair as they landed in the middle of the farmyard. 'We got hit this morning. Marmaduke's last act of betrayal. We were lucky; it looks worse than it is. Thankfully, the bats were already at their stations by the cliffs and gave us just enough warning to evacuate, and the pigeons were mostly on errands. Now, I need both of you on high alert. Marcus, get airborne immediately. Your squadron is en route to intercept bombers spotted over Rye.'

Marcus saluted. 'Yes, sir.' He turned to Linus. 'Good luck, Linus. I pray to Zeus we'll see each other at the day's end.' The two birds shook wings and the majestic falcon soared into the sky.

'What about me, sir?' asked Linus. 'I take it I'm on spotting duty with the rest of B-Squadron?'

'Are you mad?' answered Butler. 'I need every able-winged flyer I have out there today, and from what I've been told you are fast becoming quite the ace. There is some bad news though. Follow me.'

The buzzard led Linus into the sick bay. It was full of birds, mice and woodland creatures who had been hit by the early morning raids. To his horror, at the back of the room was Atticus, lying on a mossy nest, his head bandaged and his wing in a sling.

'Atticus! Are you OK?' Linus flew straight over to him.

'Oh, don't worry too much, little bird,' the old goshawk smiled as he awkwardly tried to sit up. 'I got hit good and proper this morning, so I'm out for the count today. I'll be back right as rain before you know it. Please just . . . take good care of my squadron.'

Linus was confused. 'What?'

'Linus, you've become the fastest, most skilled flyer we have, as good as any peregrine. It's time for you to step up, take charge and look after our mob. You got that?' Atticus tried to smile through the pain.

'Yes, sir!' he saluted. 'I won't let you down.' And in his heart, he knew he wouldn't.

'Good lad. Now, I'd better get some rest before the doctor grounds me permanently.'

Linus left his old mentor and followed Wing Commander Butler back outside.

'I need you to cover any human planes flying in from the Channel to the east of here. Harass, annoy, hold up and, if possible, sabotage them all. Any questions?'

'No, sir,' Linus replied.

'I appreciate I might be leaving you a little light-winged, but it's not all bad news. I've drafted someone in, someone who I believe you might be acquainted with,' Butler said.

Linus turned to see B-Squadron, or what was left of them, with a new recruit.

Ava!

Linus could barely believe his eyes. He rushed over and fell into her wings, his heart exploding.

'But? How? When? I was starting to lose hope!'

Ava held him tightly, and he could feel her tiny heart beating fast. 'No time for all the details now, baby brother.' She pulled back and smiled at him. 'But the short story is: I broke a wing.

A very kind seagull rescued me from the plane that we downed, and nursed me back to health. She saved my life, but I've been on sprats and sardines for weeks – yuck! So, Squadron Leader, what are our orders?'

Linus looked at his rag-tag squadron. Two cocky marsh harriers, a cheeky magpie and a very tired-looking owl – and his beloved sister, thin but very much alive!

They were the misfits, and that was exactly where he belonged. Confidently, he took charge.

'OK, we're not the most . . . conventional fighting unit, but let's work to our strengths. Ava and I will scout ahead and get eyes on the enemy. Now, we can't just rely on poo; no matter how much we trust in it, we'll all run out of it sometime so we need something more. Pico, I need you to scrounge anything you can find – pebbles, rocks, shells; the sharper the better.'

'Easy. I've got some crab mates on the local beach who can help us there.'

'Great. Victor, Vera, you grab handfuls with your powerful talons, then we attack the enemy planes with all we've got. If we get the speed and angle right we'll shatter their windscreens. At worst, we'll put them off course, which should make them sitting ducks for our boys. Tyrone . . . TYRONE!' Linus shouted at the owl, who had nodded off.

'What, sorry? Bit tired, but raring to go . . .' he said with a yawn.

'Tyrone . . . you just . . . make yourself useful.'

'Roger! Peck me if I nod off,' he muttered to his magpie friend.

Butler squawked from across the farmyard. 'From the bats! We have incoming enemy aircraft over Folkestone!'

'B-Squadron, get airborne now! SCRAMBLE!' boomed the Wing Commander.

'You all know what to do. Good luck!' chirped Linus, and with that he and his brave sister took flight.

The bats' radar was spot on. As the pair reached Folkstone they could see the shadowy shapes of three German bombers coming in over the sea.

'Heinkel He 111s,' Linus screeched to his sister. 'Get the others, now!'

Ava turned and alerted the rest of the squadron, who returned armed with claws full of sharp rocks and stones. Minus Tyrone.

'I don't know where he is,' Pica explained. 'We got to the beach and he disappeared. If he's run off like a coward . . .'

'We don't have time to worry about that now,' said Linus, flapping his wings to hover in the air. 'Look, here's what we do. We get in front of them, gain some altitude, then dive-bomb the windscreens. Release your payload at the last minute, then pull up and fly like the wind to get out of there. These guys aren't stupid. If they cotton on to us, they'll train their guns on us. Trust me, I know from experience. OK, ready? Let's go!'

The squadron flew hard into the wind, gaining altitude. It was tough going and every one of them felt the strain and the effort

before they'd even got to the right height. Circling there for a few seconds to catch their breath, they then arched their wings and barrel-rolled over to begin their dives. Linus could see the bombers a few hundred feet below, getting ever nearer.

'Closer, closer . . .' he whispered to himself. 'NOW!'

He released the sharp, jagged stones from his tiny feet and, remembering his training, banked hard. Once he had gained altitude he turned to see . . . nothing. His stones had bounced harmlessly off the cockpit of the German plane. He circled and watched on in horror as one by one the birds in his squadron took aim, with perfect accuracy but little effect.

'Linus, we have to do something,' said Ava. 'We've got one last run and then the Heinkels will be free to bomb their target.'

The birds gathered their ammunition and then once again climbed as fast as they could before rolling into a dive and unloading their ammunition on to the huge bombers. But as Linus feared, once again their ammo all bounced off harmlessly. It wasn't working. He shut his eyes in frustration. It was too late – the bombs would drop and they would have failed. As he opened his eyes to witness the inevitable, he was attracted to movement across the sun. It looked like hundreds of little black specks were getting bigger and bigger . . .

'What is that?' he yelled to his sister.

'It's Tyrone!' shouted Ava excitedly. 'And I think he's brought some friends!'

The owl smiled and saluted from afar.

'*Mon ami!*' The familiar sound of a French-Canadian accent

pierced through the wind. 'Your owl friend found us when he was searching for stones. You only had to ask and we would answer!'

'The geese! Thank you, sir – and way to go, Tyrone!'

'Little swift, you might be a little crazy, but you have heart, no? Geese, on my command, follow me,' ordered Wing Commander Pierre Boucher of the Canadian Geese Squadron.

As one, the huge squadron of geese soared into the sky, then, banking hard, dived straight at the German planes.

'It's now or never!' muttered Linus.

Expertly waiting until the last second, Pierre released the buckle carrying the cargo of stones on his undercarriage and veered away. The stones hit the cockpit of the German plane and SMACK! They could hear the windscreen crack, as if a bullet had pierced the glass.

One after another, each goose hit their aim perfectly.

'They did it!' chirped Linus.

Sure enough, now unable to see properly, the bombers were in total disarray. One went to turn for home, and although two carried on it was clear they had no idea what had happened or where each other was, and were flying badly out of formation. Just then, the birds heard the familiar sound of Merlin engines over the white cliffs below.

'The Spitfires! The RAF are here!' cheered Pico.

The sleek fighters made to intercept the trio of bombers and picked them off with ease, one by one.

'It works!' said Linus. He turned to his squadron. 'Get word to any able-bodied bird who can carry stones and get them ready to fly. This is how we beat them!'

13

For years to come, any animal or human would remember where they were and what they were doing on that fateful day.

Once the birds realised they could slow the bombers down with a combination of stones, shells, sticks and the tried and tested method of poo, a system was set up involving help from all the land animals. From the mice of the ground crew, the local forest and town dwellers, squirrels, stoats, foxes, pet cats and dogs, to even the birds in the sick bay, they assembled on the beach to help load up any animal who could fly with as many rocks and stones as they could carry. Then, after being alerted by the bats' radar and guided by Linus and Ava, they followed the geese and dropped their payloads on top of the hapless German bombers.

Chaos reigned and rained! The German pilots were confused

and bewildered but also angry. The day was not without loss for the birds, however. Several times Linus saw geese, kestrels and a few seagulls stray too close to the propellers of the enemy or get shot down by a stray bullet and disappear into the Channel below.

But as the day wore on, and even though the Germans kept coming, it was clear the Allies were destroying more aircraft than they were losing.

As dusk began to fall, the exhausted birds of B-Squadron and

their friends seemed to have done enough. The skies were clear.

'That's it, there can't be any more today. Let's head for home,' Linus ordered.

As the birds turned back, something moving against the sea below caught the swift's eye. Ava also saw it, and knew exactly what it was.

'Linus, there's a Spitfire down there and he's in big trouble.'

She was right. A lone plane was heading for home, but it was

dropping in altitude and was far too low to make it over the cliffs ahead of him.

Thinking quickly, Linus shouted orders to B-Squadron. 'Ava, go and get Marcus and the rest of A-Squadron. Pico, get the bats! The rest of you, tell every bird able to fly to follow me!'

With that he dived towards the stricken Spitfire. His idea was a long shot, but they had to give it a go.

Flight Lieutenant Ginger Thomas had fought long and hard all day and he was exhausted. Everything had happened so quickly, from scrambling from his tent, getting the plane into the air, in formation, and then . . . contact! The whole sky had gone crazy, full of planes, both German and Allied. One second he was soaring through the clouds, a German fighter or bomber in his sight – FIRE! The next, the planes had all disappeared and he was flying through deserted azure-blue skies. Then he would land, eat whatever he could get his hands on, try and get some rest sitting on a camp chair by the hangar, and then the call would come again: 'Scramble!' He'd lost count of the

number of German planes he'd shot down.

He had no idea if they'd won the battle or not, but he'd seen wave after wave of German planes come, and, to his relief, he was still here.

He'd spent most of his day dogfighting over the Thames Estuary. The Germans were relentless, bombers and fighter escorts all aiming for the docks. But with daylight fading, Ginger was certain they'd call off the bombing raids, and he was ready to head for home.

But then he saw that one last straggler, a stray Dornier making for the safety of the French coast. Ginger weighed up the odds. He had enough fuel, and was pretty sure he'd got enough ammunition, so he went for it. Dropping in behind the German bomber he rattled off a barrage from his Browning machine guns and saw a smoke trail coming from the back of the Dornier. Ginger looked around him to get his bearings as he started to head for home. It was then he saw it . . . The German Messerschmitt coming out of the clouds behind him. He cursed his foolishness. He was out of ammo, and the German had him in his

sights. He threw the Spitfire all around the skies, but the pilot behind him was good. He heard the bullets whizz by him as he tried desperately to shake the enemy, but he couldn't run for ever. He heard the sound of bullet on metal and he knew he'd been hit. Looking around to assess the damage, he knew the best he could do would be to try and crash-land, but the German would surely finish him off before that happened. He waited for the inevitable . . . But there was nothing. Looking to his right, he could see the Messerschmitt heading off to France. Had the pilot run out of ammo? Short on fuel? Ginger didn't care - he was alive! Now, however, he had a whole different set of troubles.

Getting his bearings, Ginger could see he was about half a mile off the coast of Dover. With the light fading to the west, he didn't fancy putting his beloved new Spitfire down in the sea, but he was losing altitude fast, and those white cliffs that had welcomed him home so many times were now looking deadly.

Linus was first to catch up with the Spitfire, just as Ava, Marcus and the rest of A-Squadron arrived.

'What on earth can we do?' Marcus asked desperately.

'Get under the wings,' Linus instructed his friends. 'We'll all lift together and carry him over the cliffs.'

'What? Are you crazy?' shouted Marcus over the wind. 'We'll never be able to do that – it's too heavy. It would take a whole flock of birds!'

'Just as well I'm so popular!' grinned Linus. 'Look behind you!'

The falcon turned to see the sky full of birds – geese, buzzards, all of B-Squadron, the bats, the pigeons, Wing Commander Butler and even Tyrone the owl.

'I DID say I was nocturnal, NOT lazy,' the owl replied to Marcus's look of disbelief.

'Everyone, get under the plane, and on my command, lift!' Linus ordered. 'Three, two, one, NOW!'

Working together, the birds flapped their wings and strained against the weight of the mighty Spitfire. At first it seemed to be in vain; the plane was too heavy.

'Keep pushing!' Linus screamed.

Slowly,
gradually, the nose
of the plane started to point upwards from the sea,
towards the middle of the cliffs at first, and then it kept rising,
higher and higher until, as the grassy cliff edge came into view,
the plane just made it over, skimming the grass on the top.

Ginger couldn't believe what had happened. Somehow, against all the odds, his little Spitfire had done enough to get them home over the white cliffs. He extended the landing gear straight away and safely touched down on the green, green grass of the cliffs' edge.

As the plane came to a halt he pulled back the canopy and climbed out on to the wing.

In the glare of the setting sun, he looked out over the Channel to see the sky full of birds, all different types, soaring, swooping and making such a noise . . .

If Ginger had been a superstitious man, he would have sworn they were welcoming him home.

He'd never seen a more beautiful sight.

Epilogue

'Attention!'

Flight Group II stood to attention as Wing Commander Butler came out of the door of the now-repaired farmhouse to address his flyers.

'At ease! Now, birds, the battle may have been won but the war is still very much alive. And our role is more important than ever. There are night-time raids happening in London and we need to be on high alert.

'A-Squadron, are you ready?'

'Sir,' replied Marcus.

'B-Squadron, ready?'

'SIR,' replied Linus. He looked to his side, Ava next to him and his loyal squadron behind him.

'Then—' The Wing Commander stalled as a starling burst out of the farmhouse door. 'The bats have picked up movement over the Broadstairs coast, sir!'

'Righto. A and B Squadrons, move to intercept,' the buzzard ordered. 'Good luck!'

'SIR!' the squadrons answered as one.

The farmyard became a hive of activity as the birds prepared for take-off.

Linus flew over to Atticus. 'Now, Master Linus, I don't want you fretting today, first day on the job. B-Squadron is yours now. I'm retired! I'm strictly a trainer from now on. You'll make a better Squadron Leader than I ever was.'

'That's rubbish, Atticus, but thank you.'

The old goshawk shook Linus by the wing. 'Remember: you're a swift. Be proud of it!'

Linus looked over to Marcus.

'Sure I can't tempt you over to A-Squadron?' said the falcon with a playful smile. 'I could use a good wingman!'

Linus looked around at the collection of misfits behind him, all loyally waiting for his orders.

'Afraid not, my friend. I'm right where I belong, but tell you what. How about we race you there!'

Author's Note

The 15th of September 1940 would go down in history as one of the most important dates in the Second World War. It is now known as Battle of Britain Day. By keeping control of the skies, the Allies made it impossible for the Germans to stage a land invasion (known as Operation Sealion). It is widely regarded as one of the key days that led to the Allies winning the war.

This book is dedicated to Tom 'Ginger' Neil and to all the men and women of the RAF from every nation, who fought so bravely to win the Battle of Britain.

What's the big deal about the Second World War?

Dermot O'Leary is fascinated by history, but he's not a professional historian. To help him get some of the details right in *Wings of Glory*, his friend James Holland – the author of many books on the Second World War and the presenter of history podcast (for grown-ups) *We Have Ways* – read the book before it was published.

JAMES: Why did you decide to set your book during the Battle of Britain?

DERMOT: As a child I loved everything to do with history. I grew up in the east of England, where there were still so many airbases from the Second World War, and as an adult I've become completely fascinated by the era. I'm in awe of the bravery of ordinary people, pulled into extraordinary circumstances beyond their control. I've enjoyed learning about everything from the uniforms people wore, to the planes that were used, the incredible codes that were created and broken, and the amazing acts of courage of people on both sides who were living normal lives until the war hit.

And how about you, James, what makes the Second World War so interesting to you?

JAMES: It's very similar for me! I didn't learn about the war at school, but one day I saw a Spitfire plane in the sky near where I live and wanted to find out more. Amazingly, the very next weekend there was an air show at the Imperial War Museum – I went and was hooked! Even though it's quite recent history, it can still be hard to imagine what people's lives were like. I often wonder whether I would have been a soldier or a pilot or a sailor, and how I might have handled living through such an enormous event. It's all the human experiences of the past which are most interesting to me.

DERMOT: I'd love it if you could tell my readers a little bit more about the pilots involved in the Battle of Britain – who were they?

JAMES: The short answer is a LOT of people! The Royal Air Force from the United Kingdom was joined by volunteers from 13 other nations. At that time, women didn't fly during battle (it would be different now) so the pilots were all men. We know that those in the RAF were very young – on average just 20 years old and some were as young as 18. Can you imagine that?

And finally, one last question for you, Dermot: what about the real-life animals of the Second World War – do you know anything about the part they played?

DERMOT: There were SO many animals who played a part in the war. There were dogs who found injured soldiers during battles, pets who led their owners to shelters during air raids, cats who kept military boats free of rats and many, many fearless pigeons who delivered messages, and inspired some of my own characters!

It's hard to pick a favourite story, but I was particularly impressed when I learned about a brown bear called Wojtek, who was adopted as a cub by Polish troops. He eventually grew to be taller than your average human soldier, and much, MUCH heavier. But he was tame, and he was given the rank of Private so he could help during fighting in Italy. He carried ammunition to help supply front-line troops, and became a bit of a local celebrity! Wojtek moved to Scotland after the war and lived out his retirement at Edinburgh Zoo.

Acknowledgements

When you sit down to write children's fiction set in wartime, you want to get it right, both in tone and historical accuracy. To be both respectful of the past, and to engage a new generation. Yes, it's fiction, but I wanted Linus and his company to educate and inform as well as entertain. So, my eternal thanks to my two long-time editors, Sarah Lambert and Kate Agar who have helped me shape this world. They've been my constant wise counsel, emotional support (everyone needs an emotional-support editor) and all-round good eggs.

Ditto for the excellent human that is Alison Padley, who makes every room and every page sing with her unique grace and enthusiasm.

Thanks as always to Ruth and the whole team at Hachette for making me feel at home and welcomed into the family, one that I'm so happy to be a part of.

Sincere thanks and appreciation to Claire Powell, who has done an incredible job at bringing Linus and the crew alive. I couldn't have imagined them looking any more brilliant – thank you so much. I hope this is the first of many 'War Tails' we can work on together.

My deep gratitude to James Holland and Al Murray, who have taken me under their Lancaster-sized wings, and have always encouraged and indulged my gloriously amateur obsession with all things WW2.

So, too, Matt Jones, a dear friend and travelling companion, who also happens to be a Spitfire pilot . . . I know!

To dear Geoffrey Wellum, Eric Carter and Tom 'Ginger' Neil, all of whom sadly passed, who gave me so much of their precious time in the winter of their lives, with good grace and infinite patience.

And to Tom's son Patrick, who made me an honorary member of the Neil family one very special summer.

To my parents for fostering in me a love of history, reading and curiosity.

And to my wife Dee and my son Kasper, they are my north star.

JOIN TOTO THE NINJA CAT AND HER BROTHER, SILVER, AS THEY BEGIN THEIR FIRST ADVENTURE IN LONDON. THEY'VE JUST MOVED TO THE BIG CITY FROM A TINY VILLAGE IN ITALY, AND THEIR NEW FRIEND, CATFACE, HAS BEEN SHOWING THEM AROUND. BUT DANGER IS AFOOT - READ ON TO FIND OUT MORE . . .

As the cats stepped off the Tube at Camden Town, not far from Regent's Park, it was clear that the parakeets had good reason to be hysterical. What had been a sleepy, tranquil night was now pandemonium. There were animals everywhere! The local dogs were barking (which in animal language is just shouting the same thing over and over again) and trying to get out of their gardens; the neighbourhood cats were hanging around the street corners, chatting loudly and looking moody. Birds of all sorts – blackbirds, pigeons, robins, tits – were swooping through the sky, making more noise than the rest of the animals put together. Even a couple of hedgehogs had emerged from a nearby bush, looking a bit sleepy and confused.

CAMDEN WAS IN ANIMAL CHAOS!

'Robert, what on earth is happening?' Catface asked a passing parakeet.

'You sure you want to know?' the bird replied, perching on top of a gate. 'It's the zoo. We flew over there about an hour ago, and the whole place is in uproar ... **BRIAN HAS ESCAPED!**'

CHAPTER 4

'**BRIAN? ESCAPED? BRIAN? HOW CAN THIS BE? IT'S IMPOSSIBLE!**' ranted Catface, his face sheet-white.

Toto and Silver looked at each other blankly. *Brian?*

'This is a disaster! We'll have to evacuate the whole of Camden now!' Catface continued. 'Thank you, Robert. Best of luck, eh. Are you heading out of town?'

'Don't worry about me,' chirped Robert. 'I've got these bad boys,' he said, flapping his wings. 'I can fly – Brian can't. It's you guys who need to worry – he'll be coming this way for sure. I'm off to squawk at more animals!'

'This is bad, kids, as bad as it gets,' said Catface. 'We are in deep doo-doo.'

Silver fell about laughing. 'Deep doo-doo! Brilliant. Toto, he said *DOO-DOO!*'

'My friends, you don't understand,' said Catface. 'We *have* to get you two safely home. Then I must be on my way, back to my family to warn them, and then I think I might make for the country ... high ground – Scotland, perhaps. I've got more family there. I can get the morning train and be there by lunchtime ...'

'I'm sorry,' said Toto, 'but **WHO IS BRIAN?** And why is everyone so scared of someone called ... *Brian*?'

'Listen very carefully,' said Catface. 'You have no idea what Brian is capable of. He's clever, he's silent, and he is almost impossible for humans to catch. Brian is the stuff of legend, a ghost story that mummy animals tell their kids to make them behave. "*If you don't eat all your dinner, Brian will come and gobble you up.*" Only it's not a made-up story, it's true! If he comes this way, which he will, as there are so many of us to … *gobble* … we're all doomed. We have to get you inside.'

'But what *is* Brian?' asked Toto.

'Brian,' sighed Catface, 'is a snake. And no ordinary snake … He is the famous King Cobra of London Zoo, one of the deadliest snakes in the world. Everyone has feared this day from the moment he was given a home there. Now that he has escaped, he will eat whatever he finds: birds, snakes, you, me. He will then try to mate and have babies—'

'UGH, GROSS!' exclaimed Silver.

'Thanks for that,' continued Catface. 'If he finds a lady cobra, and there are many in captivity around London, they will have forty or fifty babies, and do you know who *they* will eat? **ALL OF US**.'

'But … he's called *Brian*. He doesn't sound *that* scary,' said Silver.

'I know,' replied Catface. 'It's a ridiculous name. I'm sure it was given to him to make him sound a bit cuddly and friendly, two things he absolutely isn't. Now, back to your house, you two, and don't come out again until he is caught.'

'You said he's impossible for humans to catch. Why don't we have a go?' asked Toto.

'Have you taken leave of your senses?' asked Catface. 'He's one of the most dangerous animals on the planet, and you want to go off on some adventure to find him? And just suppose we do track him down, what then? I can't fight him – no one can. We have to get to safety *now*.'

They trudged back to the house where they had started their night-time adventure only a few hours before. Catface was about to help them over the gate, when Toto turned around, a steely look in her eye.

'Listen,' said Toto. 'This is your home, right? If you run now, you'll never come back. We've just got here, and we love it already. Yes, it's a bit cold, and your pasta is nowhere near as good as ours, but look at this street. All the animals live happily alongside each other. This is our home and I for one want to fight for it. So I'm not running away—'

'Sis, you can't run away,' Silver interrupted. 'You can't see where you're going.'

'Not helpful,' replied Toto. 'But yes, I wouldn't actually be able to see exactly where I was going, thank you, Silver.'

'You're welcome,' he said.

'So, what's it to be, Catface? Will you help us, and will you let us help you?'

Catface sighed, and smiled at the two little cats. 'Look, I'm a coward. I don't like fighting, and there is no way – **NO WAY** – we can defeat the awesome power of Brian. But if you insist on trying to capture him, then … oh, I can't believe I'm saying this … then I'll help. We'll have to start at the zoo to find out where he's headed. Oh my, we're all going to get eaten!'

'Keep it light, Catface,' said Silver. 'So, you're in?'

'I'm in,' said Catface.

'Good,' said Silver. 'Because we have no idea where the zoo is.'

Catface, of course, knew exactly where to go.

DERMOT O'LEARY is the bestselling author of the *Toto the Ninja Cat* series, which has sold hundreds of thousands of copies and been translated into sixteen languages. His extensive career across the television, radio and entertainment industries has established him as a household name. Dermot is currently seen presenting ITV's *This Morning* alongside Alison Hammond every Friday. When not entertaining viewers through the telly, Dermot can be found via the radio waves as he kicks off the weekend for listeners on *The Dermot O'Leary Show* on BBC Radio 2. He's fronted shows including *The X Factor*, *The NTAs* and *The Earthshot Prize Awards*, a BAFTA- and RTS-winning event that was set up by The Royal Foundation. He has always been passionate about history and has fronted and produced documentaries such as *Battle of Britain: The Day the War Was Won*, *Return of the Spitfires* and *48 Hours to Victory*. When he's not got his head in a history book, he enjoys time with his son and an afternoon at the Arsenal, or a nice wild swim.

CLAIRE POWELL is a *New York Times* bestselling children's book illustrator, who has worked on many chart-topping books with authors such as Kes Gray and Simon Farnaby. *The Swifts*, written by Beth Lincoln, was an instant *New York Times* bestseller and *The King's Birthday Suit*, by Peter Bentley, was nominated for the Lollies award in 2023.